The Mariposa Club

Also by **Rigoberto González**

Camino del Sol: Fifteen Years of Latina and Latino Writing (editor) (2010)

Men without Bliss (2008)

Butterfly Boy: Memories of a Chicano Mariposa (2006)

Other Fugitives and Other Strangers (2006)

Antonio's Card (2005)

Crossing Vines (2003)

Soledad Sigh-Sighs (2003)

So Often the Pitcher Goes to Water until It Breaks (1999)

The Mariposa Club

Rigoberto González

Tincture
an IMPRINT OF LETHE PRESS

First published by Alyson Books in 2009.
This edition published in 2010 by TINCTURE, an imprint of LETHE PRESS, INC.
118 Heritage Avenue • Maple Shade, NJ 08052-3018
www.lethepressbooks.com • lethepress@aol.com
ISBN: 1-59021-350-5
ISBN-13: 978-1-59021-350-6

This is a work of fiction. Names, characters, places, and incidents are products of the author's imagination or are used fictitiously.

Set in Minion, Marker Felt, and Market.
Interior and cover design: Alex Jeffers.
Interior illustrations: iStockphoto.com.
Author photo: Deidre Schoo.
Cover photo: © Monart Design - Fotolia.com.

LIBRARY OF CONGRESS
CATALOGUING-IN-PUBLICATION DATA
available upon request

For the young mariposas we all once were.

For the young mariposas who are, and will be.

For Lawrence King, our fiercest mariposa.

PART ONE

September Sadness

The Fierce Foursome

The girls—yes, it's what we gay boys call each other—are already sitting on our designated planter, the one farthest from the Senior Quad, which was our choice and not anyone else's. Isaac, the only white boy among us, is also the only smoker, but that's because he has an after-school job at his father's jewelry store at the mall and can afford the cigarettes. Trini bums one or two on occasion, especially when she's on the verge of some anxiety attack, which is often since anything from a math quiz to a pimple can push her over the edge. Liberace—yes, as in *that* Liberace—and I don't even touch the things. Lib, our own delusional overweight beauty queen, because he doesn't want to stain his teeth since he hopes to go into politics someday and "white teeth are essential for television appearances." And me because both my grandparents died of cancer, and so did my mother. So sucking on a cancer stick is not as sexy to me as it is for Isaac who sits cross-legged on the corner of the Queer Planter, ogling the jocks through the lenses of his dark glasses.

This generic block of cement with nothing planted in it because we live in the desert and the school needs to conserve water has been our gathering spot since we started hanging out together. We dubbed it the Queer Planter soon after. We wanted to make it official and paint the name on it but Principal Beasley—that's Boozely behind his back—made up some excuse that it was defacing school property and that if he allowed that to happen then the next thing we knew we'd be swimming in graffiti, which would be an improvement on this vomit-colored brain-dead institution of lesser learning we call Caliente Valley High School.

Freshman year we weren't the Fierce Foursome we are today because yours truly wasn't out to himself yet, and Trini had still to transfer from our rival high school in the next town. She was moved to CV High because she almost got herself killed by showing up in drag to Homecoming.

"What the hell took you so long, Maui?" Trini says. "We're like, in a state of crisis here, trying to figure out if we want to highjack the Prom Committee or the Senior Trip Committee."

"Easy," I say. "The Senior Trip Committee."

"Told you," Lib says, flicking his finger at Trini's shoulder.

"But the Senior Trip Committee is all of one or two snapshots with the cell phone and the Prom Committee is, like, the most influential part of the most important night of the year," Trini argues. "I mean, guys lose their virginity at midnight and girls get pregnant two minutes later. What do you think, Isaac?"

Isaac shrugs his shoulders. "I don't care," he says. "I can't lose my virginity ever again or get pregnant so what do I care about prom night? And I sure as hell can't bake in the sun like the rest of you Mexican girls, so I'm not going to lobby for a trip to the beach, either." Isaac lifts his chin and massages his throat as if he's helping the smoke slide down.

"So, to summarize," says Trini—and we all know this is how she begins to express her discontent—"you all are going to help

Rigoberto González

make this the most miserably boring year of my miserably boring life."

"Drama queen," Lib sing-songs.

Trini takes a deep breath. "I mean, this is our last year together in this godforsaken town and in this godforsaken school. We already spent three years in the trenches, girls, crying into each other's shoulders, sneaking around the parking lot at Menagerie, hoping some drunk will pick one of us up—"

"Yeah, that was a time to remember," Lib chimes in, and I'm certain we're all transported to the night Trini came up with the bright idea to wear our most provocative clothes and stake out a gay club in Palm Springs. The closest we got to any action was when a guy came over and hurled all over Lib's shoes.

"But we did it together," Trini insists. "We're the Fierce Foursome. We have to do something to get into the yearbook. Otherwise no one will remember we were even here."

"I'm looking to forget," Isaac says.

"Oh, you shut up, Miss Sour Grapes," Trini snaps, "Right now white girls should be seen and not heard. What about you, Passion Flower?"

I'm so used to hearing Trini take up most of the airtime that I'm caught by surprise. And when she calls me Passion Flower, I'm reminded of how I came out to myself in the first place: four years ago, Trini sashayed into freshman algebra class with faint traces of makeup over her dark complexion and plucked eyebrows.

Mr. Howard said, "I know you were a few chapters ahead in your old algebra class, Trinidad, so you'll have to be patient with us."

"That's all right," Trini said in a voice so loud and feminine that I cringed. Her head swiveled side to side on its neck. "I'll let ya'll catch up."

The Mariposa Club

I felt the group ridicule gather, but I wasn't part of it. I admired the bravado, the fierceness. I knew I wanted to be just like her. Three years later I'm nothing like Trini, but she gives me something to aspire to, that's for sure. That's also why "he" is a "she" twenty-four-seven and not only when we're the Fierce Foursome. *She's* definitely the fiercest.

"Well," I say, "I think there's another way to make sure we have our photo op for the high school yearbook."

"Oh," Trini says. "How's that? Joining the Drama Club—you know it's the only theater company in the history of the world not to welcome fags."

"Screw the Drama Club or any other school club," I say. "I just came back from doing a little research. Did *you* know that we only need five office-holding members to start our own club?"

"Okay," Trini says. "Are they going to let us count Liberace's tits as two? Because there are only four of us here."

"Maybe we can count your mouth," Lib retorts. "It's certainly large enough."

"Or maybe we can count my dick," Isaac says, and that stops the conversation because we've all seen it in the locker room. It's what gets the rest of us any respect around here—the fact that we hang around (interesting choice of words) with the most endowed member (here we go again) of our high school.

"Uhm," Trini says, temporarily shell-shocked. "Anyway, so what's your plan, Einstein?"

"The plan," I say, "is to form like CV High's first-ever LGBT club, and to put it down in the books for future generations of queers. It'll be like our precious victory *and* our greatest legacy."

"I'm still waiting to hear who's going to be our fifth member," Trini says. At this point it's clear she's pissed she didn't think of it herself because it's brilliant. "Although we know there are, like, a hundred more homos at this school, they're all closeted."

"I said LGBT," I say. "That means we can invite a dyke."

Rigoberto González

We sit there, mulling it over for a minute or two before Lib speaks up. "Okay, I'll say it: Maddy."

As if on cue, Maddy comes lumbering down the sidewalk with a yellow slip of paper in her hand. Maddy, one of the few black girls in the school, is as big as football player. She gets thrown out of a classroom at least once a week because she doesn't take any shit from anybody, but she can't get tossed out of the school itself because her father is the town sheriff. So, she gets sent to the principal's office, where a big chair is brought out for her to sit out the rest of the class period.

"Yoo-hoo, Maddy," Trini calls out. Maddy looks at Trini as if she wants to break her in half.

"Can you let me handle this?" I say. I'm not Maddy's friend exactly, but my older sister used to babysit her when she was younger, so she spent a night or two at my house back in the day. Like me, Maddy also comes from a single-parent home. I used to fantasize that she and her father would move in with us because Maddy's father is hot and I'd still kill to see him in the shower.

"Maddy," I say. "You want to join our new club?"

"What kind of club?" she yells back, all the while she keeps walking by.

"An LGBT club," I say.

"What's that? A sandwich club?" she says.

"Good grief," Lib says.

"A Lesbian-Gay-Bisexual-Transgender club," I say.

Maddy pauses and stares me down. "Do I look like a queer to you?"

Isaac can't hold back a snort.

"I ain't no damn lesbo," she adds.

"She's not?" Lib whispers.

"I know you're not," I stutter, though I too am confused. My gaydar, I suddenly realize, doesn't work across genders. "But we need a fifth member to get something started here."

The Mariposa Club

"Oh, forget her," Isaac says. "She's not rebellious enough for us. She couldn't handle being part of the biggest 'F.U., CV High' moment of the decade."

Isaac's reverse psychology works like a charm. Maddy's face forms a sheepish grin. "I'm in," she says, and then lumbers off to the principal's office.

"Good work," I tell Isaac.

"What?" Isaac says, "I actually meant it."

"I still don't think it's a great idea," Trini says.

"Which?" I ask. "The club or Maddy?"

"Both," she says. And on that note, the buzzer announces that senior/junior break is over. We all go back to our designated classrooms—Isaac and I to honors calculus, Trini to general calculus, and Liberace, who's the only junior among us, to the front office because that bitch tested out of third-year math when he got, like, the highest score in the county on the PSAT when he was just a sophomore.

"I think your idea is awesome," Isaac says.

When he's away from the other two, Isaac is actually the warmest person. He lets his guard down. We also have this crush on each other that we've been ignoring all this time, but that's part of the pact among the four of us: no sex or dating drama. We have sleepovers and lie next to each other all night like sisters, despite the rumors circulating that we suck each other off on weekends, weeknights, and between classes. I mean, we watch gay porn together and surf the hook-up sites together but that's all in good fun.

"Thanks, Isaac," I say. I have the urge to put my arm around him but that would look strange on all counts: I wouldn't want him to misinterpret the gesture of affection, and I wouldn't want some asshole homophobe to ruin the tenderness of the moment with one of those knowing sideways glances that annoys the crap out of me. Although the entire school knows what we're mostly

Rigoberto González

about, there's still a little Maui inside me who's afraid people will find out that I jerk off at night thinking about Mr. Trotter—that's Hotter behind his back—the young history teacher who was hired last year to replace Mrs. Parker—that's Barker behind *her* back—the old dog who retired because she was so senile she couldn't even find her homeroom in the mornings.

"Hey," Isaac says before we follow the stragglers into the classroom, "keep me company in the store after school? My father's making me work the front counter while he does the numbers in the back on weekday afternoons. The mall's pretty dead."

"Sure," I tell him.

I follow Isaac into math class. Mrs. Lemmons—that's Melons behind her back, or rather, Melons front and center—rolls her eyes at us. "Any day now, boys," she says, and I'm thankful that there's no way the jocks in the room are going to take their eyes off her chest to even bother looking at Isaac and me take our seats in the back row.

Melons starts in on the hour-long lesson and I zone out suddenly because calculus isn't that big of a deal. And since Isaac's catching up on the reading for English class, I imagine he thinks so too.

It's not that I don't appreciate that Isaac is good-looking. He's the tall, blond, blue-eyed white boy that broke every girl's heart as soon as it became common knowledge what team he played on when he latched on to Trini and me, sophomore year. Our then baby freshman Lib came sniffing around soon after, more interested in Isaac than in the concept of safety in numbers. Before then Lib was content disarming everyone with his size—no one wants to beat up a big girl. He had no interest in Trini, and sometimes I suspect he still doesn't, because Trini makes Lib feel invisible again with her over-the-top public persona. Isaac and I let those other two fight it out on the stage; we're content keeping a low profile.

The Mariposa Club

Personally, although I have sex in the brain most of the day, I don't think I'm going to do anything until I find the right guy. Yes, go ahead, have a laugh. I'm seventeen and still a virgin. "Maui the Catholic Girl" is what Trini calls me, the unplucked Passion Flower. Besides Isaac, the only person I'd give it up to in a heartbeat is Hotter, but he's so vain and self-absorbed he hardly even notices the rest of us. My purity is such an old joke now that it rarely comes up anymore. That's another reason Trini feels superior to all of us, she's actually had sex, many times, or so she brags. And when Lib tried to claim the same Trini shut him up with, "Oh, don't even try it, big girl, we all know your pussy's on your face." Geez, no wonder Lib dislikes her.

Although Isaac says he's had sex he doesn't like to talk about it much. It's like Murphy's Law: the most desirable one in the room is the one who doesn't show a libido. Even my sister Mickey—that's short for Micaela—thinks Isaac's hot and always hangs around when I have him over. And once it's clear that Isaac doesn't have time for her either, she goes off with her community college friends. My father, on the other hand, tries to stay away when Isaac's around. He works late anyways, but he'll call ahead or make a lot of noise at the door before he comes in from Las Cazuelas, where he's the restaurant manager. It's like he's afraid he'll walk in on a blowjob-in-progress or something. Really, Papi.

But then, I don't blame him. Once Isaac and I *did* get close to doing something. It was one of those strange full-moon evenings when Trini and Lib didn't bicker and decided to drive up to Palm Springs for spring break without us. It was only thirty minutes away but Isaac and I had wagered that they'd kill each other by minute five. We stayed behind because we thought it was stupid to cruise around the streets without being able to get into any of the homo bars since, *hello*, we're still underage and look it. The two of them put on makeup and wore see-through tops and off they went to haunt the parking lots for action. And since my

Rigoberto González

house was emptier than Isaac's, we rented a few DVDs and had a sleepover.

It was awkward at first because we stripped down to our undershirts and boxer-briefs, and although we had seen each other naked in the gym, there was a strange sensation of intimacy that night, me in the kitchen keeping an eye on the microwave popcorn and Isaac fumbling with the remote, a can of soda in his hand. I couldn't help myself from checking him out, and after I sat down next him with a tub of popcorn on my lap, I got aroused when he reached in to grab a handful.

When we're alone, Isaac is quieter, maybe even sad. I suspect there's a hurt in there, but he won't reveal it. I should know. I walked around like that for years after my mother died when I was twelve. There I was, the shy kid who had withdrawn into himself even more than before just as I had grown comfortable with who I was because my mother loved me that way. And now that my mother was gone, so were my confidence and that feeling of security. Then Trini came along and I knew it wouldn't be so bad after all. I mean, if she can walk around the way she does and even have people like my father be comfortable around her, well, there's hope for me and for anyone.

But Isaac, beautiful boy Isaac, has both his parents, business owners who expect their handsome oldest child to take over the jewelry store one day. He's the oldest of five, and the rest of his siblings are girls—all of them looking like cookie-cutter versions of their homely mother. Mrs. Dutton wears a tired expression all the time, as if she spends her energy breaking up fights between her son and her husband. As for Mr. Dutton, he's still resentful that the only male in the bunch turned out to be, well, you know. That's why I'm the only one of the Isaac's friends who's allowed in their house or even in their store. The flamboyant Trini and the effeminate Lib are not welcomed there. Not that they care, but it does hurt Isaac's feelings.

The Mariposa Club

We were talking about such things that night, ignoring the television, which was playing some forgettable action flick at low volume, when suddenly the room got quiet. Maybe it was the way the sadness took shape on his face, maybe it was the fact that his chest was looking hot beneath his tight undershirt, maybe it was the full moon, or the warm desert air, or the soft accidental grazing of our hands when we reached into the popcorn at the same time. Whatever it was, next thing we knew the tub was on the floor and Isaac's mouth was pressed against mine and our arms around each other felt so comfortable and good.

"Mauricio," Isaac whispered, and my name sounded so sexy because I had never heard him say it. It was always Maui—the shy gay orphan. But Mauricio was capable of kissing another guy and loving every second. It was my first excursion into the art of tongue wrestling. That's how Trini always gauged her interest in a man: "I would tongue wrestle with him," she'd say, nodding her head once.

And to think how far we would have gotten if my father hadn't come barging in like an immigration raid! In that split second between the door knob turning and the door opening, Isaac and I managed to pull our bodies apart, pick up the tub of popcorn off the floor and turn the volume up on the DVD to pretend we were into the action hero and not into each other. My father wasn't fooled, though, even after Isaac mustered up the most in-nocent-sounding "Good evening, Mr. Gutiérrez." And so, after that, my father always made sure to announce that he was com-ing in, although Isaac and I agreed not to go there again, for the sake of the Fierce Foursome.

"For the sake of the Fierce Foursome," I say in a low voice as I look over at Isaac behind his desk, looking so cute with his face over a copy of *Pride and Prejudice*. He turns to look back at me and winks. My breath stops.

Rigoberto González

At the Lame View Mall

Isaac's the only one with a car. The rest of us are too poor for wheels, although Trini's always taking out her Aunt Carmen's ancient gold-colored station wagon with wood paneling on the side that she affectionately named Paulina Rubio, "because, like the pop singer, she's also a Mexican blonde." That's how she and Lib drove to Palm Springs on that infamous spring break weekend. The other part of the story is that they got busted for driving around without a license or insurance. Trini still refuses to get a license but her elderly aunt won't nag her about it because she depends on Trini to drive her to the market and to the doctor and stuff. Trini blasts Britney Spears at full volume on those cheap speakers that will one day explode. Poor Aunt Carmen—I bet she had no idea what she was getting herself into when she agreed to take Trini in so that Trini could change high schools.

The saving grace is that we all ride with Isaac to school most of the time, which spares us the humiliation of riding the yellow school bus. I think Lib is the only one who doesn't mind either

way. He lives in the housing projects for the farm worker families so he doesn't even pretend he's not where he's from. Though
where his grape-picking parents came up with a name like Liberace is kind of a great story.

It turns out Lib's parents used to be part of this heavy-duty religious group, some branch of Christians that prays and preaches
to the point of flinging themselves to the ground. When the kids
started coming—conceived in, and then born into this state of feverish passion—Lib's father decided to get clever with the names
and use them as yet another way to witness. The first child was
named Encomiéndate, which asks people to surrender themselves
to the Lord; the second was named Reconcíliate, which asks that
they then make peace with the Lord; and the third was supposed
to be, quite simply, Libérate, as in achieving spiritual liberation
or bliss. But something got lost in the transfer of information, or
maybe it was just a typo, but in any case, Libérate García ended up becoming—quite fittingly it turns out—Liberace García.
Though to all of us, including his parents, he's simply Lib.

Well, it's not that Lib's older siblings do anything with the names
either. They're hard to spell or pronounce in either English and
Spanish, so in the outside world—as in, outside of their parents'
home (they now exercise their faith in a less severe church)—
they go by Ennie and Celie. Ennie, Lib informed us, married one
of those white girls from the trailer park across the tracks and
moved away to some horrible place like North Carolina.

Celie, well, she's the cool older sister I wish I had. I mean, I
love Mickey and all but she's too conformist—a straight girl
through and through. She's all about makeup and diets and gig-
gling around the boys and fantasizing about weddings and hon-
eymoons. Celie, on the other hand, is an institution at the Plain
View Mall—that's *Lame* View to us. She's the first person that
catches your eye when you enter because she's the Goth Cop,

Rigoberto González

Lame View's resident tough-cookie security guard, inch-deep in white-face and pitch-black eyeliner.

As the girls and I parade into the front mall, there, keeping the peace at the Hot Dog Factory is Celie—a veritable contrast in dark and light.

"Hey, sis!" Lib calls out and she beckons him with her finger, the nail painted deep black. "Okay, what does she want, another coat of charcoal on her lips?" Lib complains. "I'll catch you bitches later."

"Hello?" Trini says. "You're not going to leave me stranded here all by myself, are you?"

"Just come with me," Lib says.

Trini rolls her eyes. "Well, after we're done running errands for Madame Celie, over there, I suppose we'll catch up with you girls later tonight at McMurders or something. Gotta eat!"

"Call me on my cell," I say and Trini flips me the bird because the only one of us with a cell phone is Isaac.

"Well," Isaac says, "to the grindstone."

Joyería Dutton is located in the corner of the center of the mall, which makes it difficult to ignore. In this working-class town it's the place people come to buy cheap bling on layaway. Isaac says all of the pieces on display are floor samples. When a customer actually picks one out, Mr. Dutton orders it from the warehouse.

"What if someone wants it on the spot?" I asked.

"Not the expensive pieces," Isaac said. "The cheaper shit we've got sitting around by the bag in the vault."

When we get to the store, a Mexican couple is looking over the cheaper shit. Mr. Dutton stands over them, speaking in his strange Spanish. His voice soft and seductive because he wants to make the sale, no matter how small. Isaac once told me that his grandfather, a Scottish or Irish immigrant, had changed the family name from Duttenhofer to Dutton, to sound more American and fit in. It's interesting how Mr. Dutton has to make yet another transformation, changing the store name from Dutton Jewelry to Joyería Dutton, to fit into the mostly-Mexican southern California.

"Ah, mis hijos," he announces and the couple looks back and smiles at us.

"Hola, Mr. Dutton," I say. "Buenas tardes," I say to the customers.

"Buenas tardes, joven," they reply and then turn back to the row of bracelets, long and thin as angel hair pasta.

"Hey, pops," Isaac says as he moves to the back of the counter.

After we drop our backpacks in the back room, Isaac glances over the sale logs and I pick up the cleaning rag and the spray bottle to wipe off the glass on the display cases. I picked up this chore without pay on my own since it gave me something to do while Mr. Dutton switches roles with Isaac. As soon as he's off to count numbers, Isaac relaxes and we can have a regular conversation again.

The Mexican couple makes their purchase, we say our polite goodbyes, and as soon as they're out of earshot Mr. Dutton's tone changes.

"What took you so long, Isaac?" he demands.

"What?" Isaac says, "I was only, like, five minutes late."

"Five minutes mean nothing to you? Is this how you will run this business? Five minutes behind everyone else? Don't make me scold you in front of Maui," Mr. Dutton says as he takes the logs and scurries to the back.

I can't help but blush at Mr. Dutton's mind games. We all know it's something else that bothers him, namely, that Isaac has never had a girlfriend. And never will.

"Asshole," Isaac says.

"Hey," I say.

Rigoberto González

Isaac raises his hand and says, "Don't bother. I can't even feel it anymore."

Feel what? I want to ask him. His heart? But *I* can, I want to say. Instead, we do what we have been trained to do—we go numb, we make jokes, we pretend we're so much Diva we're made of steel and nothing can touch us. Isaac rubs the back of his neck and then he moves on. We both do.

"Oh, my God, will you look at that?" I say, grateful to be able to point out a distraction.

Trini and Lib are carrying a piñata shaped like a giant—well, it's supposed to be like one of those Renaissance-inspired swords or something—but there's no mistaking a penis when one sees one.

"Suck on this, bitches!" Trini calls out.

"Hey! Less talk, more action," Celie yells from the other side of the piñata, but since we can't see her it sounds like it's coming from the penis itself. "We're shoving this inside the truck."

"Mercy!" Trini yells.

"We'll catch up at school tomorrow," Lib says. "We're setting up Celie's house for a Goth party this weekend. And we're all invited!"

"I guess we'll have to spike our hair and wear all black," I say.

Isaac shakes his head. "It's always something with those two."

For the next hour or so we stand around and talk to potential customers. If somebody actually wants to buy something pricey, Isaac calls Mr. Dutton from the back, but nothing great goes down this afternoon so we don't see Mr. Dutton again until closing. The only action we usually get is watching Celie escort members of Los Calis out of the mall because they're being obnoxiously loud. Los Calis are the Caliente Valley's dope-dealing, petty-thieving Mexican gang. But this afternoon, not even the gang members came to the mall.

"Slow today," Mr. Dutton announces, matter-of-factly.

The Mariposa Club

"I'm going to drive Maui home," Isaac tells Mr. Dutton.

"Yes," Mr. Dutton responds, disinterested.

We pull down the security barriers while Isaac's father locks up the display cases inside. "Another day, another duller," Isaac mumbles.

"Don't worry," I say. "Your days are numbered here," and as soon as the words slip out of my mouth I get chills. It suddenly dawns on me that the Fierce Foursome will break apart as soon as we graduate. Where will we go? What will we do? Will we stay in touch?

"What's the matter?" Isaac says. "You look pale as butt."

"I just had a crazy thought: we're all going to split this banana we call Caliente Valley High," I say.

"Oh, geez, you're not going to get all cheesy are you?" Isaac says. "For us queers that's a good thing. We hate high school, remember? And it hates us."

"Isaac!" Mr. Dutton calls out suddenly.

"Give me a minute, will you?" Isaac says to me and then walks over to his father.

I know this part of the relationship all too well: it's the scene where Mr. Dutton yells at his son for not doing something perfect. Mr. Dutton gets all emotional and red behind the barrier, which seems to keep him from reaching over and grabbing Isaac's neck. Isaac simply stands there, one foot taller than his father but getting smaller by the second, until it's over.

"Is that all?" Isaac says, loud enough to show me that he hasn't been broken down completely.

"I'll talk to you at home," Mr. Dutton says, and turns away.

We get to Isaac's little Honda Civic and climb in. The car faces Lame View Mall. The stragglers are dragging their feet out to the sidewalk and a few cars are slowly making their way out of the parking lot. Everything here moves at that pace, like a slug booger.

Rigoberto González

"And so what?" Isaac says, continuing a conversation I had no idea we were still having. I can hear the anger building up in his voice. "What are we going to leave behind, anyway? This stupid town of Caliente, California, and our stupid school and our stupid teachers and our stupid families."

"I happen to love my family," I say defensively, and I immediately regret it.

"Oh, yes, excuse me, I forgot," Isaac says. "Little Maui loves his daddy and his big sis. Excuse me for hating my stupid-ass father and my stupid-ass mother. Excuse me for living—"

Isaac drops his head to sob inside his arms over the steering wheel. I'm not sure what to do. This is the part that we never figured out in the Fierce Foursome, how to be affectionate with each other without feeling weird. It's always ha-ha-ha and hee-hee-hee and then when something serious comes along we're clueless.

I let him exhaust himself with crying, and then his body relaxes after the release.

"I'm sorry," he says.

"*I'm* sorry," I say. "I feel like such a dipshit just sitting here not knowing what to do."

"That's because we can't do anything yet," Isaac says. "We're not even high school graduates. We're not even eighteen years old. And we're queers. We're invisible. We're nothing."

"No, that's not true, Isaac," I say. I reach over and hold his hand. "We're friends. We matter to each other."

But I can't help but feel there's a truth to what he just said. It feels more palpable suddenly as the parking lot empties and we're the last vehicle left standing, alone and silent in the deserted asphalt. The cars driving past on the avenue might not even care to notice us, but there we are—two seventeen-year-olds on the cusp of adulthood and the overwhelming freedom that comes with it.

The Mariposa Club

Trini's Drama

After Isaac drops me off at home, I stand at the driveway for a minute, thinking about how complicated our final year of high school's going to get, when Mickey comes rushing out of the house looking like she's wearing a lamp shade over head to protect the proud beehive she has worked on all week for the retro-party at the community college.

"Oh, my God, Maui, get over here!" she screams.

Knowing that my sister is one of the biggest drama queens on the block, I don't quite see through the urgency of her tone. I'm thinking she misplaced her car keys or something. But then I see that her eyes have widened to a shape I have seldom seen before.

"Papi?" I ask. My body stiffens.

"Trini has been calling non-stop," she says. "His Aunt Carmen's in the hospital. She fell!"

"Seriously?" I say since I can't picture Aunt Carmen getting done in by anything, let alone something as everyday as a fall.

She's a tough old lady who used to be an actress in Mexican movies back in the sixties. "Nothing glamorous like romance or adventure flicks," Trini said as she showed off shots and stills of Aunt Carmen in green neon knee-high boots from forty years ago. "She did tons of those go-go dancing films."

"Is she all right?" I ask.

"He wouldn't say," Mickey says, and she's digging into her purse for the car keys. It's clear that Trini has asked for me, and that Mickey has already agreed to take me to the hospital.

On the way there, Mickey informs me that she's only dropping me off. She had promised to give a friend a ride to work. "I'll tell Papi to come pick you and Trini up after work," she says. "I'm sure he can stay with us tonight."

So much remains unspoken in those few sentences, that I'm grateful my sister is the understanding type. And that so will my father be about having Trini over. What neither of them has to say is that Trini can't go back with her parents. Her father all but disowned her after that incident at homecoming. Trini, fierce and fearless, decided to run for Homecoming court, and no one caught that the gender-ambiguous name, Trinidad, was not a girl but that queer kid who walked around the school in eyeliner and dressed in girl's sweaters, until it was too late to do anything about it. It became a joke that all the other outsiders and popularity rejects enabled as an affront to the jocks and school princesses. Everything had been engineered all the way up to the announcement of the king and queen, when Trini would walk up to the stage in an evening gown. But as soon as the jocks got wind of it, they cut her catwalk short by rushing her behind the stage and breaking her arm and two ribs.

For Trini's parents, who thought they had long ago grown accustomed to their outrageous only child, showing up at the hospital to find Trini broken-boned in drag was too much. So, in the guise of fearing for her safety, they had her transferred to the

Rigoberto González

neighboring high school and living with Aunt Carmen, the old eccentric relative who decades before had pranced around for the camera doing the mash potato.

When I walk into waiting room, I see Trini's father sitting on the far couch, pretending to be asleep. Trini stands glassy-eyed next to the water cooler. They look so much alike—same thin frame, same full set of hair—that not even a stranger would have been fooled into thinking they were not here together.

"Hey," I say, and Trini rushes over to bawl on my shoulder. Her father opens his eyes but just sits there, unmoved by the display of emotion.

"Let's get out of here," I say, tugging at Trini's shirt.

"Thank you for coming, Maui," Trini says, "Oh, look at me, my makeup is running! I was going mad crazy here all by myself."

"Where's your mom?"

"She's in there with Aunt Carmen," Trini says. "She kicked me out of the room and I could tell Aunt Carmen didn't like that, but she has no choice, she can't speak."

"What happened to her?"

"I think she had a stroke," Trini says. "When Celie and Lib dropped me off in front of the house, I noticed the lights were off, which is rare because Aunt Carmen loves her afternoon novelas, you know, the ones with those beefcake Brazilian actors and oh, my goodness, look at the doctor over there in the glasses, he's hot—"

"Are you frickin' kidding me?" I shake Trini by the shoulders. "Focus!"

"I'm sorry," she says, her face wrinkling with grief. "This is all too much for me. First I walk into the house and see my poor Aunt Carmen looking like she's dead, and then I have to call my parents and they start accusing me of not taking care of her! I mean, I take great care of her. I make her dinners, I drive her to her appointments. It's not my fault!"

The Mariposa Club

"No," I tell Trini as we walk further away from the waiting room. "It's not your responsibility or your fault. Aunt Carmen adores you. She would never blame you for anything."

"Try telling my parents that. The first thing they did when they got here was take away my keys to Paulina Rubio," Trini says. "Oh, Maui, I'm so scared. What's going to happen to Aunt Carmen? What's going to happen to me? I can't live on my own. Oh, my God, they're going to take me to one of those third-world orphanages and force me into child labor or something. I can see it now, the label in the back of Kate Winslet's Oscar gown: Made by little orphan Trini while sewing with no light. Do you think she'll thank me in her acceptance speech at least?"

"Trini, get a hold of yourself, you're acting stupid."

"I can't help it. You know I talk like this when I get anxious."

Just then my father walks briskly through the sliding front doors.

"Maui, Trini," he says. "Are you two all right? How's auntie?"

"Oh, Mr. Gutiérrez," Trini says. "It's horrible. She can't talk or walk and she can't even open one of her eyes anymore. My parents are in there, but—"

My father nods, "I understand. Why don't you and Maui wait for me in the car and I'll be right out."

Trini and I look at each other and then turn to watch my father take those same brisk steps toward the waiting room.

"Is *your* papi going to beat up *my* papi?" Trini asks.

"I hope so," I say. "I mean, if that's okay with you."

"Well, by some bizarre sense of Mexican loyalty I have to object," Trini says. "But my inner queen says, *You go, Mr. G.!*"

We walk past the receiving desk, where the receptionist tries to hide the fact that she's talking into her cell phone. The autumn air outside is cool and it reminds me of the times I had to take my mother out for a walk. She had been diagnosed with breast cancer, and part of her afternoon routine to get out of her depres-

Rigoberto González

sion was an exercise regimen, usually a stroll around the block. She died this time of the year, which hurts still, especially when things like the clear southern California sky in September come around to remind me.

My father's car is the nondescript Cadillac parked all wrong. For this I have another reason to be grateful to my sister—she taught me how to drive. She learned from her friends because my father is the most absent-minded driver in the town of Caliente. We don't have to decide where to sit because my father's passenger front seat is crammed with special menus and invitations to the upcoming banquet at Las Cazuelas. I had already volunteered the Fierce Foursome to help seat and serve. Only Trini of course, scoffed at that, until she found out we got to wear Mexican folk costumes.

"Dibs on the china poblana," she announced. I have yet to break the news that only male costumes will be made available for the festivity and that she won't get to wear the sequined dress with the seal of the Mexican flag in front.

We slide in the back and, after fifteen minutes, begin to get nervous.

"What are they talking about in there?" Trini wonders out loud.

"Hey," I say, in an attempt to distract her. "So I almost forgot. Tomorrow we have an appointment to see Boozely about the LGBT club."

"That should be interesting," Trini says. "Frankly, I don't see why you're even bothering. I mean, those losers don't even deserve our fierceness. We should do them a favor and burn the school down instead."

I chuckle that Trini's attitude is slowly coming around. "Well," I say, "I'm sure Maddy would light the match." We burst out laughing.

The Mariposa Club

"Wasn't that hilarious?" Trini says, and then does her best impersonation of Maddy: "*I ain't no damn lesbo!*"

"It's going to be great," I say, suddenly excited about the prospect. "I'll be president, you can be vice. We'll make Isaac treasurer and Lib the secretary, and Maddy will be our combination bouncer and member-at-large. I'm already envisioning our motto—"

"Wait," Trini says. "Why do *you* get to be president?"

"Well," I say. "It was my idea. Check. I'm putting in all the paperwork for it. Check. And if we held an election, I'm sorry, Trini, but no disrespect to you but I think I would win by a landslide. Check."

"Uncheck: two or three votes is a landslide to you?" Trini says.

"Compared to none, yes." I say.

Trini purses her lips. "Well, I'm so pleased to know that the democratic process is alive and well as evidenced by this self-appointment going down at C.V. High."

"You're joking, right?" I say. "You want us to run against each other in front of our three voting members?"

"I'm only saying it's a tad presumptuous to say that I could not be elected president over *you.*"

"And all I'm saying is that maybe voting members don't want someone in office who doesn't even notice that anyone else might have something to say because she does most of the *talking.*"

"Mauricio Gutiérrez!" Trini yells out. "I am shocked and dismayed that you should insult me in the parking lot of JFK Medical while my poor old dear aunt is in there bedridden and I'm sitting here crying my eyes out in the back seat of your father's *car!*"

I have to roll my eyes at that one. "And I am devastated that you should manipulate the situation just to get yourself the sympathy vote."

Trini clutches her invisible pearls. "Why, I do declare!" she says in her best southern belle accent.

I shake my head. "Trini, look, stop it. What are we doing?"

"We're fighting like two kitties in a potato sack?"

"That's not where we should be right now. I mean, I—"

The whole exchange halts when the driver's side door opens. My father climbs in, turns the ignition and says in the calmest voice he can muster before we gun it out of the parking lot, "Let's go boys. Trini, you're moving in with us until graduation."

"What?" I say. "Papi, what?"

Trini is overjoyed and does a little "raise the roof" hand gesture.

It turns out that the inquiry into Aunt Carmen's health took a strange turn when Trini's parents started arguing about what to do with Trini while the patient was in recovery. Certainly the kid couldn't move back home and certainly the kid couldn't live on her own since she had just turned seventeen over the summer and didn't even have a driver's license. Trini would have to be sent back to Mexico until she came of age. My father, the sensible grown-up that he was, understood A: how dangerous this would be to a gender-bending queer kid like Trini, and B: how disruptive this would be to her education, so there was a third option, C: for Trini to move into the Gutiérrez household in order to avoid both A and B.

"He's your friend, Maui," my father concludes the explanation. "And your friend needs us right now."

I'm seeing Papi in a different light all of a sudden, as if he's not as homophobic as I thought he was. "So...dealing with yet another crazy high school kid is not going to be too much for you?" I ask him, and he gives me the "we'll discuss this further later" look through the rearview mirror.

All through the ride over to Aunt Carmen's to pack some of Trini's things and all through Trini's whirlwind essentials-gathering, like her teddy bear pajamas and furry rabbit slippers, I remain numb, trying to process the idea of having to spend both day *and* night with the outspoken, overbearing, motor-mouth, Trinidad Ramos. Wait until the girls get wind of *this*!

Mickey's waiting for us on the front porch without the lampshade on her head, which makes it easier for Papi to lean over and give her a one-minute run-down of the situation.

"You serious?" she asks. Papi nods his head. "Well, welcome to the family, Trini," she says, and then just as quickly: "Though, around here, everyone pulls their own weight with the household chores. You're not a guest. And, uhm, I'm still the boss around here, squirt, since I'm the oldest."

"All in good time," my father says as he drags over clean sheets and pillows into my room.

The Gutiérrez house is a three-bedroom deal: after Mami died, the master bedroom was handed over to Mickey, who got her own private bathroom and study space. And I got the next largest room because of the desk and the side entrance to the back garden. My father took the small bedroom in the back near the communal bathroom. He didn't mind the twin bed and the efficiently-packed dresser since he didn't bother to date after my mother passed away. So he's never had any overnight guests and all he wears is one version or another of his manager's uniform.

I have a queen-size bed and an open floor, where I usually lay out the sleeping bags when I host the Fierce Foursome sleepovers. But even with Trini's lump of personal items now on display, I feel slightly invaded.

"We'll bring out the extra bed from the shed tomorrow," my father announces. "For tonight you can sleep with Maui."

"Thank you, Mr. G.," Trini says, and she runs over and gives my father a hug. My father blushes and so do I. We're a close family, but we're not into impulsive PDA.

Rigoberto González

Once my father leaves and shuts the door behind him, Trini says, "Well, here we are."

"Here we are," I say. "Look, Trini, about the whole incident back in the car—"

"Forgotten," Trini says. "I need some privacy. I want to change into my teddy bears."

I turn my back to her, though this is quite silly. We have seen each other naked in gym class, back when we had to take P.E., before Boozely allowed us all to opt out for the sake of our queer safety and their straight comfort. But now that I remember, Trini never did change for P.E. She got out of it from the get-go when she informed the school counselor that being around jocks in the locker room gave her post-traumatic stress since she was attacked at homecoming.

"Okay," Trini says.

When I turn around I'm nearly floored. Trini stands in front of me in the nude, but covering her privates. A large burn, long-since healed, lies splashed across her chest, the nipple has been left discolored and misshapen. Satisfied that I have seen the front, Trini turns around to show me her back side, where a cigarette burn has been nailed in from the middle of her spine.

"Oh, my God, Trini," I say. "Your father?"

Trini nods her head and reaches over for her pajamas and slips them on. "And my grandfather, back when I was younger."

"Why did you show me these now?" I ask.

"Because I'm grateful that for the first time in my life I'm with people who don't want to hurt me," Trini says.

"What about Aunt Carmen?" I say.

"She does her best to protect me."

"Geez, Trini, I'm so sorry." But words don't seem to do this moment justice. If anything it makes me feel that much more of a jerk for being mean to her about the whole LGBT club presidency. It also makes me realize how fortunate I am that I don't have to deal with my father the way Isaac has to deal with his, or Trini with hers. No one gets to choose their parents, their high school, or their community. And if you're one of the unlucky ones, life will be one big frickin' burden after another. The only consolation I can offer Trini is a hug. I walk up to her and put my arms around her.

We stand there for a minute, my body leaning on hers more than the other way around because I want her to forgive me more than anything else.

"It's okay," she whispers, and then caresses my shoulder.

We crawl into bed and turn off the lights. I can hear the intensity in Trini's breathing, but when I listen more carefully I realize that it's coming from me.

"Thank you, Maui," Trini says. "I'll be on my best behavior. I don't want to disrespect your family's generosity."

"Oh, don't worry about any of that, girl," I say. "You just be yourself. Here, we like you exactly as you've always been."

"In that case, when the second bed comes in tomorrow, I get the one with the view of the garden," Trini says. And then she adds, her voice buzzing like a mosquito in the dark, "And I get to be president."

I swat the bug away. "In your dreams," I say.

Rigoberto González

The Mariposa Club

"Oh. My. Goddess!" Lib squeals when he hears the news that Trini has moved in with my family. "Five dollars you kick her to the curb by Halloween."

"Lib," Isaac groans. Trini winces.

We're at the Queer Planter before classes start. The sky is overcast though I don't try to read too much into it since we have an appointment to see Boozely during study hour. First, however, we want to resolve the issue of the office holders. I show the group the requisite form and explain that we can make a better case for the club if we present it to the principal already filled out.

"Wait," I say. "If we're going to do this right then we have to have all our voting members present."

A silence descends on the group.

"Good luck roping Maddy in," Lib says. "She comes to school on her own schedule."

But for the second time, as soon as her name is invoked, Maddy makes an appearance.

"Uncanny. It's like chanting Bloody Mary," Trini says, and then waves at her. "Yoo-hoo, Maddy!"

Maddy's eyes narrow as she slowly makes her way over. It's not that she isn't agile or even smart. I remember in junior high, especially, both Maddy and I were part of the academic *and* athletic decathlons at Woodrow Wilson. We would even study and train together on the weekends when she spent them at our house since her father had those long shifts at the precinct. Ah, the gorgeous Sheriff Johnson. He's still something of a catch, and unlike my own widowed father, he's quite a ladies' man.

I suspect that has something to do with why Maddy became the way she is—deliberately defiant of her natural talents. She started losing interest in sprinting and in spelling as soon as Sheriff Johnson started dating one of the school secretaries. The kids started making fun of her and asking her to pimp her new mommy out for hallway passes. It wouldn't have been half as bad if Sheriff Johnson didn't make such a public display of the whole thing, hand-delivering a dozen roses on Secretaries Day and stuff like that.

In the end, that secretary came and went, and so did a string of other love interests. I always knew about his love life because my father brought it up at dinner sometimes.

"That Raymond Johnson," he would say, with no small hint of jealousy. "Brought around a beautiful Asian lady to the restaurant for lunch. One of those new gals at the bank, I hear."

It must be difficult for my father, a homely restaurant manager, to watch how a police officer who rose so quickly in the ranks to became sheriff also became the city's most eligible bachelor. And it must be hard on Maddy, who got big and held back a year in school, to watch her father move from flower to flower like the hardest-working bee in the hive.

"What do you bunch of sissies want from me now?" Maddy says. "I've got to get to the library."

Rigoberto González

"You read?" Trini asks. I roll my eyes.

"Look, you better watch yourself, Trannie," Maddy says and Lib bursts out laughing. "You too, Glib," she adds.

"Never mind them, Maddy," I say, trying to keep the peace. "Listen, we're electing officers to the LGBT club and we need your vote."

"Okay," she says, "I vote for myself."

"All righty, then," Isaac chimes in.

"Well," I say, waving the form in my hand. "That's not exactly how it works. We've got to fill in these little slots."

Maddy snatches the form. "Don't condescend to me, Bow-Wowie," she says. And then it hits me—it's Maddy who came up with all those nicknames for people, from Boozely to Melons. Not Hotter, though, that one just named itself.

"I'd like to be money-keeper," Maddy says. "I'll collect dues and break kneecaps on late payments." She takes out a pen from the back of her ear, writes in her name on the line naming the treasurer, and then gives me back the form.

"Sounds like a match made in heaven to me," Isaac says.

Trini stomps her foot. "Well, if we're just going to call it then I call president."

"No effing way," I say.

"Order, order," Lib says.

Trini turns to him and says, "Hey, who made *you* president?"

"Girls!" Isaac says. "First of all, it says chair in the form, not president, so let's get off that label train ASAP."

"Chair?" Trini scoffs. "Can't we at least call it something more interesting like 'divan' or 'chaise longue?'"

"Look," I say. "We can be co-chairs, is that all right, Trini?"

"I suppose," she concedes. "Though it doesn't sound quite as influential now."

"Which one of you wants to be secretary?" I ask, and Isaac and Lib point at each other.

The Mariposa Club

"Oh, come on," I say. "It's no big deal. You get to take down minutes at the meetings and stuff."

"I can't spell worth a shit," Lib says. "Besides, I'd rather do something a little more dramatic, like publicity. I'd be perfect for that. I'm all about spreading the word and telling it on the mountain, you know me."

I write Lib's name down. "That means you get to be secretary," I tell Isaac. "Learn it, live it, love it."

"Yippee," Isaac says, flatly.

"Okay, now comes the important part: what are we going to name the club?" I ask.

"How about the Fierce Foursome, what we've always been?" Lib offers.

"Hey, math girl, did you also forget how to count?" Trini says. "There are *five* names on this list."

"Then we can be the Quite Fierce Quintuplets," Lib says.

"What are we now, a singing group? Lame," Trini says.

"Then you come up with something, your majesty," Lib says, pointing at Trini with his chin.

We stand around for a minute contemplating names: The Diva Delightfuls (Trini's idea), the Caliente Hot Babes (Lib's), Valley Girls (Isaac), the Rainbow Crew (mine), Britney's Queers (Trini again), the Hagless Fags (Lib), the Sun Queens (Isaac), The Out and Abouts (mine again), Madwoman and the 'Mos (Maddy, though it did get a chuckle out of us) and finally, after explaining to Trini that the Fire Island Fairies is not even within the realm of our West Coast reality, she nails it.

"How about The Butterflies: An LGBT Club," she says. "You know, it's what they call us homos south of the border—fluttering butterflies!" Trini bats her eyelids.

"Ooh," Lib says. "I actually like it."

Rigoberto González

"Me, too. It's got flair, some nice metaphor potential—an out-of-the-cocoon thing going on. So then let's vote on it since we have like a minute left before the bell rings," I say.

"The Butterflies," Trini says, breathing deeply. "As in *mariposas*. What do you think, Mads?"

Maddy sniffles and then says in her deadpan voice, "Then keep it in Spanish, dummy. The Mariposa Club. This is Mexican country, ain't it?" And she walks off, leaving all of us stunned.

"Genius," Trini says. "*How* does she do that?"

The bell rings, shaking us out of our bliss coma.

The final step is to name our faculty advisor, but that's a no-brainer. We'll ask the only teacher we all love: my homeroom chemistry klutz, Ms. McAllister—that's Disaster behind her back.

"Genius," Trini declares again. "So we meet you there at the end of first period!" And we all take off to our respective home-rooms.

Ms. McAllister is about five feet tall, a hundred years old and always sports an impeccable home perm dyed a shade of dark so brown that no light squeaks through it. Her class is the perfect start to the day because some mishap or another wakes us all up—always a spill, a breakage, a release of some foul fumes that forces us out of the room for the rest of the period. Her demonstrations are legendary, but so is her love of her students. In her eyes, no one can do any wrong, even when a few of the jocks make snide remarks about the Fierce Foursome, she's so sensitive to conflict that she guilt-trips the assholes into apologizing for their bullying and sweet-talks us injured party into forgiving the perpetrators. Still, she's like our great-great-grandmother who's somehow kept up with all the new developments of modern science.

This morning the hour comes to a disappointing close without an incident that gets the students tittering into lunch period. But in truth, I'm not much in the mood for laughs. I've got Isaac to think about and now Trini, and the only thing I have any control over is this stupid school club. Ms. McAllister waves her arms around in front of the periodic table and I imagine how wonderful it would be if our lives were ordered like that—by atomic number. Alkali metals on one side, noble gases on the other, and this is what happens next. And this is what happens after that. Never a surprise or a shock. Boring and predictable seems a lot more manageable than uncertain this morning.

As soon as the other students spill out through the desks and onto the hall, I rush up to the front of the classroom.

"Ms. McAllister," I say. "We have a special request."

"We?" Ms. McAllister says.

"The girls and I. They'll be here in a second."

Ms. McAllister's eyes sparkle like shiny buttons. She's adorable and always huggable, which is what Trini does as soon as she arrives, her arms wrapped around the teacher as if she might blow out of the room with the small force of our breathing. Lib and Isaac come in shortly after.

"You all want to make peanut brittle again?" Ms. McAllister says, guessing at the reason we've come. "Not until the end of the semester."

"Why don't we make something with a little more pizzazz, like truffles," Lib says and Isaac elbows him because we've got like two minutes before we have to get to our next class.

"Actually," I say, my words rushed. "We need an advisor for a new club we're starting on campus. It's an LGBT organization called The Mariposa Club."

Ms. McAllister blinks twice, soaking the news in. "Well," she says finally, "that's brave of you." She reaches into her pocket protector for a pen. "It's about time the school joined the rest of enlightened society in the new millennium."

"No kidding," Isaac says.

Rigoberto González

"Yaaay!" Trini says and kisses her on the cheek. Ms. McAllister giggles, and then the rest of us take turns giving her a peck on the cheek as we head out the door, backpacks in tow.

"Well, that was easy," Isaac says. "So what next? Convincing Boozely that it's a go?"

"Since we're co-chairs, Trini and I will speak with him during study hour," I say. "And then we'll rally during lunch to report back. See you then!"

For the second period, we all split up again because, as in math class, we're at different levels of English: Isaac is in college prep, Lib, the PSAT junior-year genius, with me in honors, and Trini is tracked in basic.

"I must confess," Lib says as we walk into the classroom. "I'm kind of excited about this."

"Me, too," I say.

We take our places in the back of the room, to the communal table that's Mr. Knowles'—Doze behind his back—attempt to keep us interacting and conversing about literature. It works at every table except for ours because we have the motley group: Lib, me, Maddy, and our other resident outsider, Snake, the old-school heavy metal white dude who doesn't look anyone in the eye, except for Maddy, to her extreme displeasure, I'm sure.

About Love

English class with Mr. Knowles runs itself. He's right out of the footage on YouTube that shows boring college professors droning on and on about history or philosophy or economics or biology—the subject doesn't really matter because the language sounds the same: ZZzzzzzzzzzzzzzzzzzzzzzzz zzzzzzz. How did we ever stumble upon this kind of video on YouTube in the first place, you ask? Curiosity. We couldn't rely on film or television to tell us the truth. The media lied to us about everything: about what it was like to be gay and what it was like to be Latino. We had seen high schools represented countless times over the years and it never came close to our reality, so we figured that if we wanted somewhat of an accurate glimpse of a college classroom, we needed to go to the source: amateur video.

"You're kidding me," Isaac said. All four of us were huddled around the computer screen. "That's what we're going to get after four years of suck-ass high school? Four more years of suck-ass?"

"That's why *I'm* not going to college," Trini asserted. "After senior year, I'm done with school."

"But, girls," I said, "What are we supposed to do then, hang around here?"

"I'm with Maui," Lib said. "Boring or not, college is not high school and certainly not this backwater town. And besides, we'll be adults. Out-of-the-closet adults. Do you know what that means?"

And we sat there nodding our heads in silence. I didn't know what Lib meant, but it sounded mythical, like one of those hot vacation spots on the Caribbean. In any case, college, suck-ass or not, was my ticket out of this sad high school life and into a more interesting one, with boys who dated other boys and parties without curfews and conversations about serious subjects like sex and life's goals that didn't turn into pillow fights. And maybe I'd get a boyfriend, and maybe I'd fall in love, and maybe I'd lose my virginity—all of those wonderful mysteries that were only fantasies out of my reach in Caliente, the southern California desert.

While Doze babbles on about the Victorian period, staring out into space, lost in his own train of thought as he holds his tortoiseshell eyeglasses in one hand, the rest of us do our own thing. Lib flips through a copy of *People* magazine hidden on his lap, Maddy text messages on her phone, Snake does the same, and I draft a few thoughts in preparation for my meeting with Boozely.

I'm confident the principal won't give us a hard time about the club. It's different than spray-painting the Queer Planter, if not more important. Every clique in school has a club, no matter how small the membership. I mean, consider the river-rafting club. First of all, there isn't a mobile body of water within a day's distance to move one of those banana boats through, unless one wants to paddle it around like a canoe. And queers, well, we don't need much except visibility—a nice full-colored photograph for the yearbook that we can all look back a decade from now and say, *There we were, we existed. And we still do.*

You exist, Lib, and so do you, Maddy. And even you, Snake. High school might want to keep us invisible, but here we are, ticking away. It suddenly dawns on me that those two are text messaging like crazy, but I'm puzzled as to whom. Who in the world could they be texting? They're both legendary loners. Snake pushes send. And then Maddy pushes send. He taps the keys and presses send. And then it's her turn. That's when it hits me: these two are text messaging each *other*. I observe them more closely for the next few minutes. I confirm my suspicion: each time they read their message, their mouths gesture toward a smile. They're incapable of smiling of course, but somehow they're communicating the pleasure of it, the naughtiness of it. Sneaky little devils.

I write it down on a piece of paper and pass it over to Lib. Lib reads my note, wrinkles his forehead. Looks over at Snake and Maddy. Looks back at me and shakes his head. I nod. He looks over again and performs his own careful study. After about a minute the light bulb goes on.

I mouth: *I told you!*

He mouths back: *Wow!* And then Lib's face softens, his eyes revealing a tenderness I have always admired about him. Of all our families, it is Lib's religious parents who are the most accepting, it seems. They don't reject him like Trini's folks, they don't abuse him like Isaac's, and they don't pretend or avoid talking about it like my father. Don't get me wrong, my father's great, but if I ever try to bring up the subject he breaks out into a sweat as if he's afraid I'm going to ask him for advice like: When is it appropriate to put out for a guy, on the second or third date? Is giving a guy a hand-job the first stop on the way to Slutville? Really, Papi, believe me, I'll spare both of us those awkward conversations. I mean, he never provided that type of wisdom to Mickey. Why would I expect him to give it to me?

Anyway, for all the religious freaks out there preaching that homosexuality is sin or even curable, there are plenty more who believe that God made us this way and so loves us just the same. Thank God. Lib's parents fall in that category. Lib has the most beautiful coming out story I've ever heard.

"So we all sit at the dinner table," Lib told us on one of our sleepovers. "And there's Celie all Gothed out in a crushed velvet cape, and there I am in one of her flowery hand-me-downs, from the days she dressed like a normal big girl, and Papi looks to his left at me, and then to his right at Celie, and I was afraid he was going to slip into one of his feverish holy-roller speeches, like the ones he gives at the Sunday harvest gatherings, but no. He very calmly informs us that as long as we keep attending Sunday services, we can dress and walk around however we like."

"Well, did he ask you if you were queer?" Trini asked. Her tone was not disbelief, but it was tinged with slight jealousy.

"He didn't ask me," Lib said. "He told me."

"*Told* you?" Isaac asked. "Like how?"

"Right after grace, on that same dinner. He served me a piece of chicken and before he handed me the plate he said, 'Son, you're what some people call gay.'"

"I would crap in my pants if my father ever got the courage to even *say* the word," I admitted.

"That's basically what happened to me," Lib said. "I froze, thinking that he was going to break the plate over my head. Across from me I saw Celie thinking the same thing. She got all on the defensive, ready to hold him back or something. And

Mami stopped in her tracks coming back from the kitchen, her face turned to stone."

"So then what?" I asked.

"So I simply nodded. I mean, what was I going to do, deny it? That would be lying to my father. I've known that I was gay since I was like, six. So I decided then and there to just admit to the truth. And you're going to love what he said next."

Lib paused for dramatic effect, and it worked. The rest of us were on our toes in anticipation.

"Papi called back to Mami and said, 'Lorenza, come join us at the table. Let's have a meal with our gay son.'"

"No way," Isaac said.

"Yes way," Lib replied. "I think I had to drink water after every bite because my mouth was so dry. I was sure that any minute Papi would suddenly wake up to what had just happened. But no, he hasn't changed his mind about it since."

"That's beautiful," I said. Trini and Isaac remained quiet.

I must admit that I too feel a little envious of Lib sometimes. He can be who he is, in school and at home. That's one notch better than what the rest of us get. I remember Mickey telling me to take down all those beefcake posters of Vin Diesel and Daniel Craig off my bedroom wall.

"Why? Papi doesn't care," I said to her.

"Yes, he does, Maui," Mickey said. "I mean, he's cool with you and all but you know how it is."

How is it? It's like the military—don't ask, don't tell. But there's nothing in there about not showing. Or like Trini says, "I don't need to ask or tell; I'll just gesture. Maybe even point." And then she turns around and sticks out her behind.

I complied with Mickey's request. Papi had been through plenty these last few years. I didn't want to add to his burdens. Though sometimes it seems silly. Especially now that Trini's going to be waltzing around with a towel turban-style around her head when she comes out of the shower. Both Trini and Lib put the flame in flamer, that's for damn sure. It's what makes them fierce.

Isaac and I, on the other hand, queen out only when we're in the Fierce Foursome, and even then we're no competition for the other two, who are like uber-queens.

Lib continues turning the pages on his magazine, stumbles upon a picture of a shirtless Mario Lopez and presses the page against his lips.

"Fag," I hear someone whisper behind me. I turn around. It's the only time I become aware that we're just a few bodies among a larger group, otherwise the other students are as invisible to us as we are to them. We don't socialize with any of the others because we don't have to. I search the faces behind me. Doze drones on and on, disinterested in the disinterested students sitting in front of him. One of them—maybe the class president in his starched blue shirt, maybe the green-eyed lead actress of every major theater production at the high school auditorium, maybe the soccer hero, his natural black curls draped over his ears—one of them hates us. Or maybe they all do.

I turn back to Lib, who's oblivious to any displays of hatred. He just lets them run down his body like a single drop of rain too small to matter, too slight to bother opening the umbrella. But me, I'm overly sensitive and obsessive. I allow the smallest bug splattered on the windshield to disturb my entire line of sight.

Fag. The word hits harder when I'm by myself, or when it's only me who hears it. When I'm part of the Fierce Foursome I'm protected by our numbers, our combined strength. But isolated I'm vulnerable, perhaps even defenseless. And then another thought distresses me: After we graduate we will lose that safety in our numbers. We will be alone and exposed all over again.

"Tee-hee."

I look up, distracted by the feminine giggle, the sound of a girl tickled by the object of her affection. Maddy. It just doesn't

Rigoberto González

compute that this big black girl who spent most of her years in high school pushing everyone else away, commanding respect through fear, should suddenly betray a lovesick turtledove fluttering around inside her.

Snake gives Maddy a flirty look through the corner of his eye and raises an eyebrow. Is this really happening? Of all the oddest couples I could possibly imagine, this one's definitely as far out as Pluto. Maddy and Snake, Snake and Maddy, the black girl and the white boy, both big-boned and angry as a pair of pit bulls.

"Pssst," I call to Lib.

Lib looks up at me, looking annoyed. I signal with my eyes. Lib narrows his to consider the couple sitting next to us. He writes something down and passes me the note.

DOES THIS MEAN WE'RE GOING TO NEED A NEW TREASURER?

I shrug. I suppose it means plenty of things, but most importantly, that anyone can find someone to love. Even Mr. Knowles here with his paunchy belly and receding hairline has someone to go home to every afternoon. The gold band on his ring finger catches the light each time he waves his hand around.

That was one of our more animated conversations one night—gay marriage. Trini is all for it. She wants to wear one of those Vera Wang numbers and arrive in a horse-drawn carriage with a few shirtless muscle boys as footmen. Isaac says we shouldn't start dreaming about anything until we have, like, oh, I don't know, a first boyfriend? I like the idea in theory. I mean, a one-on-one deal sounds like it's the way to go, and I'd like to imagine that there's a guy out there who'll only have eyes for me, though right now, in our hormone-overloaded adolescence we seem to have eyes for anybody.

Lib says that he wants his father to perform the ceremony, and that he can imagine himself with that special someone for the rest of his life, the way his own parents will probably live out theirs, in the company of each other's flaws and blessings—Papi's snoring, Mami's sneezing fits in the evening, Papi's constant verbal expressions of gratitude for everything from the sun in the mornings to the breeze in the afternoons, Mami's humming while knitting baby socks for charity. In truth, the Garcías are a perfect family, and I can't help but feel a little sad that mine will hobble through the rest of time because, without my mother, we're already incomplete.

Lib suddenly looks over at me. "What's the matter with you?" he whispers.

I shake my head. The guilt stings: I feel jealous of this overweight Mexican kid in front of me who has both a mother and a father who love him very much and who accept him as a *queer* overweight Mexican kid. My face becomes a bit warm and I wonder why I'm having all of these bizarre preoccupations: graduation is nine months away—that's a very long nine months away—and so is our stepping out into the big frightening world. I've already been through puberty, growing hair in all the hidden places and complying with my urge to masturbate every day. What is it? Why am I feeling disoriented and anxious?

Snake and Maddy keep keying and pushing send. They know where they stand. They know what they want. And I can't imagine Sheriff Johnson getting weird about it since he has been running around with every pretty receptionist in the valley for the past six years or so. Besides, interracial dating and marriage isn't such a big deal anymore, certainly not in southern California. We can only hope that same-sex marriage will follow.

Lib reaches down into his backpack and brings out a small mirror with a picture of Frida Kahlo in the backing—we all have one like it courtesy of Trini's visit to Mexicali, where Aunt Carmen buys most of her meds because they're cheaper across the border. Only Lib carries it around, though, and only he would pull it out in the middle of English class to fix his bangs.

Rigoberto González

"Fag." I hear the word again. This time I see Lib look up at me, a surprised look on his face.

"What did you say?" he asks.

"Who? Me?" I say, and then my heart sinks because it's true. It was me who said it that time.

"Bitch," Lib says, and continues to groom himself, completely unimpressed and unaffected by the slip of my tongue.

Yes, Lib too knows where he stands and where he wants to be. It's *me* who's still a little bit lost, who's uncertain and scared and hostile because I have no idea what I want to do with my life. It's the Cancer in me—moody and sensitive, hard shell on the outside, soft underbelly. I just know what the next baby step is: the Mariposa Club. And for now at least that will give me immediate purpose and direction.

The Mariposa Club

Boozely

Study hour is only study hour for those of us who
get exempted from physical education. Believe me, there really
isn't anything to look forward to in the gym except the anxiety
of keeping our eyes in our head. Trini and Lib could not care less
and would stare away as if we're at the mall looking at mannequins through the safety of Plexiglas. Far from it, these chiseled
mannequins spit and bark and threaten to break your bones if
you look at them. But the novelty of nudity wears out, I'm sure,
especially with all the free gay porn on the Internet with boys ten
times better looking than some of these guys who could improve
on their looks one-hundred percent just by picking up a pair of
exfoliating gloves. The Fierce Foursome decided to spend study
hour with each other. Oh and then there's Snake and Maddy,
who sit across from each other at the back of the library and text
message the hour away. Even Mr. Gump—that's Frump, Grump,
Lump, Stump and Chump (take your pick) behind his back—
the school librarian who's as crabby as a bucket of crustaceans,

doesn't bother telling them to stop. The rest of us can't even walk in through the door wearing sunglasses without him snapping like a mousetrap.

The Fierce Foursome meets briefly at the front of the library's sliding doors.

"Showtime," I say. "Trini and I should be back before the period ends."

"That's right," Trini says. "Full report forthcoming."

"Take no prisoners, girls," Lib says. "We're keeping our fingers crossed and our legs wide open."

"Good vibes and better vibrators, bitches," Isaac says as they walk through the sliding doors.

Trini and I take long strides toward the principal's office. We've got an appointment, we've got a special pass, we've got attitude. We're golden.

"So let's strategize," I say to Trini as we make our way there. "I'll start, telling Boozely we've come about establishing an LGBT club in the school, that we've got office holders, membership, a faculty advisor, and paperwork in hand. All we need is for him to sign off and make sure it goes through without any problems. And then I'll hand it over to you and you get to talk about our mission."

"Right! CASE: community, awareness, sensitivity, and education," Trini says, reciting our statement. "I've got your back, not to worry." And then she surprises me with a hip bump before we go into the building.

"Good morning, boys," says the secretary at the front desk. "You've got your hall passes?" We wave them at her. "How can I help you?"

"We have an appointment with Principal Boo—Beasley," I say.

The secretary guides her finger on the appointment book in front of her. "You sure do," she says. She dials the principal, announces us, and then hangs up. "Go right on in."

Rigoberto González

Principal Beasley is a well-dressed, overweight man with a nice tan for a white guy. And since he never goes away during the school year (and neither does his tan), we all suspect it's one of those fake deals from the tanning salon. But none of this really matters because all anybody can notice is the combover.

There are combovers...and then there are combovers. The principal's combover drapes across his forehead with the strands all spread out like a fringe. I mean, it moves on a counter-rhythm to the rest of the body, like a tassel. It's tough not to lock your eyes on it because it's almost hypnotic, like a cobra weaving. But somehow we manage not to stare.

"What's the occasion, boys? What can I do for you this morning?" he asks, not even a sign of apprehension in his voice, though we know he hasn't forgotten our attempt from last year to label the Queer Planter.

"We've come about establishing a club," I say and then I let the sermon rip: "We feel it's time our beloved high school address the reality of the times, that gays and lesbians are everywhere, including in our halls, and that we need to have an organization in place for future generations of queer teens to meet, socialize, feel safe, and advocate for their right to be who they are without fear or resistance."

Even I'm impressed as these words are coming out of my mouth, believe me. And I sense that so is Trini. But I did my homework, surfing all the gay rights websites on the Internet with a few brief and pleasant digressions into the porn sites, of course, but hey, don't judge! I'm a virgin, remember? All I have is fantasy. Anyway, I wish I could say the same for Principal Beasley, whose combover grows flatter by the second, probably sucked in by the precipitating beads of sweat on his forehead. I finish by presenting my handy-dandy club membership sheet, filled out and signed, and then toss the ball over to my co-chair. "Trini?" I say, giving my signal.

The Mariposa Club

"Yes, thank you, Maui," Trini says. "We're all about fierceness," she begins, "and we've got plans: a drag show, maybe even a rave party on the weekends—without the drugs, of course, a float for the Gay Pride parade up in Palm Springs, oh, and Oscar night, we couldn't forget *that*. I can already picture it—*picture* it, get it?"

My body stiffens. When the hell did she come up with this? I want to reach over with my chair and stop her in her tracks before she goes too far but her motor-mouth is unstoppable.

"I see a red carpet rolled out across the entirety of the main mall," she continues. "And the yearbook paparazzi blitzing us from both sides as we catwalk up to the auditorium, which will be decked out in gold lamé and just gushing with strings of silver tinsel. It will be glitz, glamour, and gourmet apéritifs. Ginger ale in champagne glasses and a large fountain filled with glazed strawberries and naked apricots. Pucker up, my love. Oh, and look, we've even come up with our sign." Trini crosses her arms, locks her thumbs together and flutters her extended fingers. "Las Mariposas!" she shrieks. "Community, awareness, sensitivity, and education!" She stands up and throws her hands up in the air for effect.

Principal Beasley's jaw drops, and so does mine. My face reddens even more when the principal begins to stutter: "Wha-wha-wha-what is that, a gang sign?"

Trini bursts out into laughter. "Oh, sure, we're a gang all right. Except instead of drive-by shootings we're going to do drive-by shoutings: *Come and get us, boys!*"

This last line she delivers with her sultriest shoulder roll. I imagine that as soon as he kicks us out, Principal Beasley's going to hit the bottle of bourbon that's rumored to be sitting comfortably inside his desk drawer.

The next few seconds happen so fast I don't realize how we end up standing outside of the administration building again

Rigoberto González

with nothing but a faint promise of "Let me mull this over" from Boozely. I turn to glare at Trini and say, "What part of the plan was not clear to you?"

"What?" she says. "I thought it went well."

"Are you kidding me, Trini?" I unleash my fury. My periodic table of order and civility collapses, and this is the cause—Cupcake Trini and her uncontrollable urge to smear everything with frosting. "You scared the shit out of the principal! You all but told him we were turning the gym into a bathhouse!"

"Now, *there's* an idea," Trini says, pointing her finger at me.

"Stop it!" I say. "Just stop it! You ruined everything. I knew you would, you and your faggy antics. Geez, can't you have put it on hold for at least an hour while we convinced the principal that we were serious about doing something productive?"

"Well, it's not like it wasn't going to be a social organization either, Maui," Trini says. And this sets me off even more.

"That's only a part of who we are," I yell. "We're not all about rave whistles and rainbow flags, for crying out loud. We're also about making a strong statement about queerness, which includes breaking stereotypes."

"Mauricio Gutiérrez, are *you* calling *me* a stereotype?" Trini says, clutching her invisible pearls again, her jaw wide open.

"Up yours, Trini," I say and walk toward the library.

"Oh, nice," she says, chasing after me. "Why don't you tell me what's really bugging you out, Maui?"

I stop and spin on my left heel to face her. "What are you talking about?"

"You're just jealous of me, you always have been, because I'm comfortable in my skin and you never have been." This makes my face redden again. "I get to be me, no matter where, no matter what, and *you* have to hide because *you* don't want to frighten anybody—not your family, not that horrible Mr. Dutton, and not our beloved Principal Boozely. Well, I've got news for you, you

The Mariposa Club

closet cunt: I don't want to be part of your damn Mariposa club if it's going to be as lame as the other clubs whose only mission is to get into the high school yearbook. So scratch my name off your little piece of paper and leave it blank because that's exactly how it's going to stay—a big empty nothing!"

"No wonder people kick your ass," I shout, and then immediately regret it.

"What did you say?" Trini says.

She looks horrified, but I'm unable to open my mouth and take it back and apologize and admit that I let my anger do all the messed-up talking. Trini breaks out into a sob and runs away.

"Trini!" I call out too late. Though I also hear myself say under my breath, "Faggot." I shudder. Where is all this coming from? I mean, everything Trini said is true and it stings. The wound throbs so loudly I'm not sure I can simply forget about it so quickly.

As I slip into the library, I'm secretly hoping the sliding doors at the entrance will snap shut again and slice me in half. Anything to avoid having to break the news to Lib and Isaac: that the club's going to be a no-go and that I'm an asshole.

Stump sits behind the check-out counter, scolding some poor kid who dared to walk around with his iPod headphones sticking out of his shirt pocket. Lib sees me and waves me over.

"So?" he whispers as soon as I take my seat at their table.

"So, nothing," I whisper back. "We screwed it all up." I proceed to tell my sordid tale of flame-throwing and adolescent betrayal. Even the stacks of books around us seem to lean in to get the scoop. And when I'm done, the clock at the far wall seems to stretch its mouth open into a shocked O.

"Maui," Isaac says, "I can't believe this. Where is she now?"

I shrug my shoulders.

"Well, it's not like she didn't deserve a *little* grief," Lib says. "She's been getting her way all along, you know." I roll my eyes.

Rigoberto González

"Thank you, sword of justice," Isaac says. "Can we put all that shit aside for now and focus? We have to make sure she's okay. We need to go look for her."

"Hello," I say. "Did we forget we're in the state prison called high school?"

"Well, then what?" Isaac says. "Are we going to just sit here like herpes sores hoping the problem's going to go away on its own?"

"I don't know," I say. "Let me think. I can't see straight right now. I'm feeling so guilty my head hurts."

"Maybe we'll see her at lunch," Lib reassures us. "*No one* skips lunch."

"Shhh!" the librarian admonishes us from the front desk, and so we are forced to spend the rest of study hour pretending that we're studying, though Lib continues to leaf through the pages of his magazine, and Isaac and I make frequent eye contact, exchanging telepathic words of concern.

Trini is nowhere to be found at lunchtime. We split apart and stand around in the center of the chaos with our necks craned. Nothing. All of a sudden it's clear to see what this school would look like without one of us, and that it would remain completely unaffected by our absence. The river of bodies moves to its own flow, every once in a while a spurt of laughter snags the eye, but other than that, it's a creature without singular attachments. Even as we converge at the Queer Planter, our Fierce Foursome minus one member leaves us misnamed and lopsided, and the sudden amputation aches.

"It's not like she can just blend into the landscape," Lib observes, and though it's an unwelcome jab at the moment, I can't help but agree. Trini wears loud, she walks louder, and talks loudest. Without a cell phone, without a place at the school that's worthy of someone as fierce as she, we conclude she hoofed it all the way home.

"So we wait until the end of school," Lib says. "It's not like we can just take off without permission. You know that bitch is getting suspended and I have no inclination to join her. My parents would kill me. Plus, I have my future political career to think about. I *need* that squeaky-clean record."

"I can't believe you, Lib," Isaac says. "This is serious. Trini has never taken off like that before, and it's a particularly frightening time for her what with Aunt Carmen in the hospital and all."

"Lay it on thick, Isaac," I say.

"Sorry," Isaac says.

"Look," I say. "If we're going to do what I think we're going to do, then it has to be an individual decision."

"Okay," Isaac says. "So who's in?"

It's the most artificial of limitations, this inability to take off from campus when we want to because we're underaged and bound by the rules of our student status. Essentially, we've only been following the rules because that's what we've been trained to do since kindergarten. And as soon as we graduate, we're free, out of here, making the rules up as we go along. But not yet.

"We're going to break the rules," I say. "Isaac, we have ten minutes until the security guards close the gate to the student parking lot. Let's make a run for it."

"Oh. My. Goddess," Lib says. "Girls, this is the part where I feel obligated to remind you that we not only have a perfect attendance record but that we all got certificates of good citizenship last year. You should really think this over before you throw it all away. I mean—"

We're off, leaving Lib behind with his sentence unfinished because we don't have time for either the lecture or for the fifth period bell. It's actually an exhilarating sprint over to the lot and into Isaac's little Honda Civic.

Rigoberto González

"All righty, then," Isaac says. "We're going to blast out of here like the Powderpuff Girls, but where the hell are we going?"

"To Aunt Carmen's," I say. We put our sunglasses over our faces, slip a burned copy of Cyndi Lauper's "I Drove All Night" into the CD player, nod our heads in complicity and head to the hills for an all-out Diva rescue!

Casa Carmen

In the middle of the day, Caliente's a dead place, so sticking to the speed limit with Cyndi's nighttime speed-demon song comes across as slightly anti-climactic, so we lower the volume. Besides, we don't want to draw any unnecessary attention to ourselves anyway.

Aunt Carmen's house is located not far from the mall, in a small working-class neighborhood that on the weekends has at least one front yard or another decked out in birthday party balloons and one sad-looking piñata. With the kids in school it looks like a dumping ground for bicycles with training wheels and stray dogs. When we pull up to the house, a dog quickly takes shelter beneath the car, even before we get out.

The house hasn't been vacant for longer than a day since Aunt Carmen's hospitalization but it already looks abandoned. My father used to say that about houses—that they start to die without human souls. We walk up to the porch and knock.

"He's in there," a woman's voice calls out from a window in the next house.

Isaac and I look at each other. "Yes, thank you," I say. I knock again.

"The old lady's in the hospital," the voice says. "She's not there. But the fag is."

"Thank you," I say. I'm annoyed at this point and I want to say more, but the last thing I want to do is have a fight with someone I can't even see. I count my lucky stars I don't have a busybody neighbor like this where I live.

Before the voice has time to tell us anything else, Isaac tests the knob. It's unlocked. "Let's just go in," he says, and we do.

Aunt Carmen's living room looks smaller than it really is because it's crowded with furniture that doesn't match—a green couch next to a red recliner, a white ottoman, and a series of lamps, some without lampshades, that look as if they've been collected from second-hand stores over the years. Aunt Carmen's Mexican studio photographs line the walls.

"Trini?" Isaac calls out. No answer. We walk up to her bedroom.

"Trini, we know you're in here," I say. "Would you mind coming out of your room? We want to know that you're okay."

"Go away!" Trini says from behind the bedroom door.

"Trini, please," I say.

After a minute or so the door opens. Trini walks out dressed in one of Aunt Carmen's costumes—a blue flamenco dress with large white polka dots. And since Trini doesn't have long hair, the black comb rests precariously clipped to the back of her head. But the black fan hanging from a rosary bead string around her neck looks fabulous.

"Olé," Isaac says.

"You like?" Trini says, her face brightens up a bit. "It's my favorite outfit. Aunt Carmen wore this to a Mexican bullfight back

Rigoberto González

in the sixties. It caused quite a stir. Apparently the matador was so captivated by the señorita in the blue polka-dot dress that he didn't see the bull coming. He was gored and Aunt Carmen was banned from the bullfighting ring after that."

"I think you'd definitely stop traffic around here," Isaac says.

"Oh, stop flattering me," Trini says. "You're just saying that because you feel sorry for me that this brute was so mean to me."

My head drops. "Trini, listen, I—"

Trini raises her hand. "You don't have to say anything, Maui. Well, I'm being a terrible hostess. Boys, welcome to Casa Carmen. Please, sit down. What can I get you? A glass of chardonnay? A mint julep? Something to cut through the heat?"

"I'll take a glass of water with ice," Isaac says.

"Me, too, thanks," I add.

"My pleasure," Trini says.

She brings out a tray with ice water a minute later but before she takes her seat across from us, Trini opens Aunt Carmen's old-fashioned record player and puts a vinyl record on.

"Pedro Infante always cheers me up," she says.

"You know this is probably going to cost us detention," Isaac says.

"I know. And I want to say how touched I am that Maui's going to take the blame for it," Trini says.

I roll my eyes, tighten my lips, and remain mum. I guess I deserve whatever she's going to give me.

"You know I'm joking, girl, and I want to say I'm sorry too but you really did hurt my feelings, Maui," Trini says. "And you know how much I care about you. You're like the older, more conservative sister I never had."

Isaac and I look at each other. Of all the things we've adopted from the adult queer community, the preoccupation with growing older is the one that doesn't quite make sense. We're all seventeen years old and only a few months apart, except for Lib who's still sixteen. In the spring, Isaac turns eighteen. Trini, shortly thereafter. Technically, I'm the youngest of the three, turning eighteen in the summer, a few weeks after graduation. It will be another decade before we even grow our first wrinkle, and here's Trini, trying to oppress me with ageism. Silly, girl. She's been watching reruns of *Will and Grace*.

"It's hard enough as it is, what with poor Aunt Carmen in the hospital. I've never felt so alone, you know, and that's saying something because I spend so much time looking at myself in the mirror and flattering myself with compliments. I just didn't need it right now." Trini ends her speech by bowing her head slightly forward.

After a rather long and pregnant pause, Isaac kicks my foot. I react. "Trini, I'm sorry. That was a real shitty thing I said and I didn't mean to hurt your feelings, especially because you're so much my sister, we even share the same room now."

Trini sniffles. "And..."

I wince. "And what? You know, this doesn't change the fact that we still don't have a Mariposa Club."

Isaac sighs. Trini purses her lips, unfolds the fan dangling around her neck and begins to fan herself.

"You know what? Forget it," Trini says. "It's not worth it. We'll just have to deal with it when Boozely gets back to us. In the meantime, since I'm all dressed up and have no place to go, I think it would be very ladylike of you, Isaac, if you would drive me over to see Aunt Carmen. I want to take a few things to brighten up that dreadful hospital room. I mean, at the very least a set of curtains with some *panache*."

"Are you going to go dressed like that?" I ask.

"Oh, my God, of course not," Trini says. "I'm going to see my poor ailing aunt at the hospital. I should wear something a little more dignified. How about my pink silk Chinese blouse with the frog knots?"

Rigoberto González

We arrive at JFK Medical with a supply of novelties: a diaphanous scarf to drape over Aunt Carmen's IV, the record player and some classic tunes by Vicente Fernández and Lucha Villa, a black lacquer jewelry box from Michoacán, her homeland, a framed autographed photo of Julio Iglesias, a votive Virgen de Guadalupe candle, a wooden cross, a Mexican ceramic dish for her earrings, an air-blown margarita glass for her dentures, an embroidered cushion, and a pair of silver evening shoes with fierce heels that is supposed to inspire Aunt Carmen back to the dance floor. Oh, and a makeup bag.

The receptionist is too stunned by Trini's outfit to question why we're not in school and we slip through easily enough. A few people sitting in the waiting room also take notice, which is slightly annoying only because this is a hospital. I'm sure everyone here has seen more shocking things than three gay kids (one of them in drag) walking in with a few boxes full of frills. I mean, just passing by the emergency room is a quick education on how many methods can be used to stop the leak of blood.

"Aunt Carmen, it's kamikaze makeover time!" Trini shrieks as soon as we walk into the room.

I'm completely unprepared for the sight of Aunt Carmen looking shriveled up and broken, as if her body has been deboned. Her hair, usually impeccably coifed, appears nestlike, dried up, and wiry. The curtains have been drawn around the patient in the next bed over, which creeps me out.

"Hi, Aunt Carmen!" Isaac yells out, cheerfully.

"Calm down, bitch," Trini says, "She's paralyzed, not deaf."

After setting down my box next to the bed I step forward and hold Aunt Carmen's hand. She responds with a faint squeeze. Only one of her eyes can blink open, the other stays shut. Immediately I begin to tear. This is taking me back too quickly to the times I had to come visit my own mother at the hospital.

The Mariposa Club

For a gay boy, losing a mother is the ultimate loss. And I know there's all this crap out there about the domineering mother producing a gay son, but I can tell you with certainty that this wasn't the case with us. Mami was petite, a little plump, but strong, physically strong. Otherwise she wouldn't have lasted as long as she did after all that chemo. Even after the hair and weight loss, she never ceased to be Mami, the beautiful Mexican lady who loved her children so much. I imagined the pain she must have had to deal with knowing that she was going to die and leave Mickey and me behind.

It was her brains that made it possible for our parents to become part-time owners of Las Cazuelas, but when the cancer struck they had to sell their half of the restaurant. My father stayed on as the manager, which was like a demotion, but necessary, especially since Mickey and I were still too young to get jobs and help out.

Mami made it comfortable for me to be a gay boy, refusing to scold me if I clipped one of Mickey's barrettes on my hair. I don't think my father liked it very much but he never said anything. And when she started getting sick I started withdrawing, until I had sunk so low that those things that brought me happiness became forgotten.

I imagine Trini's going through something similar right now. Aunt Carmen's her Diva, just like my mother was mine. They're the women who allow us to be awkward and silly and girly without fearing judgment.

Trini leans over the bed to apply lipstick on Aunt Carmen. Isaac combs out her long gray hair.

"If you want to help, you can paint her toenails," Trini says.

"I'm not very good with that," I say, which is true, but I also feel funny about touching the old woman's feet.

"Then start putting things up," Trini says. "Just spread it all over the place so that it looks like home."

Rigoberto González

"What about Aunt Carmen's roommate?" I ask.

Trini looks over at the bed with the curtain around it taking up the other half of the room. "I'm sure she won't mind," she says.

It's déjà vu when I touch the coolness of the walls, when I get close to the sterile, odorless surfaces of the room. But the items I set up give the blankness of the place color and texture. I wouldn't be exaggerating if I said *life*. Why do hospital rooms have to look as blank as bone? I'll have to tell the girls that we might want to bring flowers next time, or maybe a plant—a purple orchid that can stand tall in the face of all this grief.

As soon as I bring out the record player, I plug it in and put one of the vinyl records on. If it hadn't been for Trini I wouldn't even know how to operate one of these old-fashioned contraptions. I'm surprised it still works. I guide the needle to the edge and soon the static takes the shape of song.

By the time I'm done, the room looks alive, and so does Aunt Carmen, who sports some light blue eye shadow and painted cheeks. Isaac has done well with her hair also. Aunt Carmen appears pleased by the changed mood of the place. Though she can't speak she shapes a smile with one side of her mouth. She closes her eye and falls asleep.

"What am I going to do without her?" Trini says in a low voice.

I turn around with the pretext that I should lower the volume on the record player, but the truth is I don't want to tell Trini what awaits her after Aunt Carmen dies.

Once you lose your Diva, Trini, the stars will blur each time you look up at them, and the bottom part of your heart will harden into lead. And for many nights afterward you will have to learn to get used to that hollow sound that is the blood screaming through that terrifying new weight that you will carry inside your body for the rest of your life.

The Mariposa Club

Behind me I hear Trini and Isaac sniffling, but I don't want to look. I have been here once before, feeling useless with my two hands that can do anything, except stop death from coming.

We sit around keeping Aunt Carmen company a little while longer, when Isaac breaks the silence. "I need to get going," he says, looking down at his watch. "My father's expecting me at the jewelry store. I don't want to be five minutes late again. Do you want me to give you girls a lift or can you find another ride?"

"Oh," Trini complains. "If only I still had my Paulina Rubio we wouldn't have to worry about hitching rides."

"We need to let Aunt Carmen rest, anyway," I say. It's something I picked up in these situations: it's a polite way to tell someone they don't have to tire themselves out.

"I'm starving anyway," Trini says. "Does Mickey cook?"

"Yeah, right," I say. "With the microwave."

We take turns kissing Aunt Carmen on the cheek.

"We'll be back real soon, Tía," Trini says, and then we file out of the room, the wing, the hospital, turning heads all the way out the door.

"So what's the plan for tomorrow?" Isaac asks. "Should we just turn ourselves in first thing in the morning?"

I sigh. "Well, we're going to have to. Otherwise we're not going to get any leverage from Boozely."

"I'm sorry, Maui," Trini says.

"Hey," I say. "Let's just move forward, okay? This day is like a fart: it stinks but the smell goes away."

"Well," Trini says. "The only consolation is that tomorrow's Friday, and if your father doesn't ground us, we'll still be able to go to Celie's Goth party."

"Oh, shit, I forgot," I say. "Maybe Papi won't be that pissed off. Let's keep our fingers crossed."

Rigoberto González

"And our legs wide open," Isaac and Trini say in unison.

Our laughter breaks the spell of grief and worry for the moment. And when we reach Isaac's car, a sense of relief comes over me. We're moving on.

Mickey's Plans

I'm surprised Mickey's home when Trini and I are dropped off. Isaac honks his horn once and pulls out of the driveway with this grim look on his face that tells me he wishes I were coming along to be the buffer to his father's aggression. But today I have to make peace with Trini, which simply means spending some quality time with her.

Surprise becomes shock when we walk into the house and Mickey's standing over the stove, sautéing vegetables in a pan.

"I thought you said she didn't cook?" Trini says with glee in her voice.

The smell of onion and green beans makes my mouth water too and I gravitate toward the kitchen.

"What's the occasion?" I ask, hoping she'll at least give us a taste if she's going to whisk the dish off to a potluck or something.

"Oh, nothing special," she says, grinning.

That's when it hits me: she wants something. And not just any old favor, she wants something huge—big enough to warrant sweating it out in front of a hot stove.

"Well, it smells delish," Trini says. "Can I set the table or something?"

"Sure," Mickey says. "Just set three places since Papi's working late at the restaurant. Don't forget, you guys, he's counting on you to help out at the annual banquet of the Latino Chamber of Commerce."

"Oh, I'm looking forward to that," Trini says, "costumes and everything."

I still haven't broken the news to Trini that no girl costumes will be available that night, but I don't want to burst her bubble just yet. Besides, there's an uneasy stirring at the pit of my stomach that tells me I'd better be on my guard during the meal: Mickey's got something up her sleeve.

As Trini does her Martha Stewart dance over the dinner table with placemats, silverware, and the deep-blue dishes, I watch Mickey carefully from a distance. Twice before she's acted this suspicious. The first time was when she wanted me to help her lobby for a family trip to Disneyland. That's the year she also changed her name from Micaela to Mickey, so I guess she wanted to do some kind of pilgrimage to her namesake's kingdom. Every year up to then our family vacation was a trip to Baja, where my mother's people are from. My father's people are from Guerrero, but he was like third-generation American, so he didn't have much of a connection to Mexico. My mother's parents, on the other hand, still lived in Baja, so every summer when they took two weeks off from the restaurant, our parents took us there. I liked going to Baja—to the beach, the seafood places, and the little outdoor porch with a yellow swinging hammock. I didn't care for Mickey or Goofy or Donald Duck. But my sister was in that phase, and so she coaxed me into whining along with her

Rigoberto González

that we wanted to go to Disneyland instead. And we eventually did. And Mickey took her picture with Mickey. Yippee.

The second time was when she had to break it to me that our mother was in the hospital. She didn't do any cooking back then though she could have, but she did wait for me outside of my elementary school classroom to walk me home. She never even liked to be seen near me so I knew something was up.

"What is it?" I asked. My tone was somber because our walk was somber, and when she told me about Mami I knew the world wasn't the same one I had woken up in that morning. Even the shadows dropping from the trees caused me pain.

So this time I'm a little more prepared. I watch in silence as Mickey serves us the vegetables with steak and brown rice on the side. She pours lemonade in the tall glasses that we only use for cold iced tea in the summers. The hot buns come out of the oven and she covers them gently with a towel before placing them in a serving basket. And then the butter is uncovered and it looks startlingly bright. She unfolds the cloth napkin and spreads it so formally over her lap. "Leave room for dessert," she announces, and then she smiles at me.

"What the hell is it?" I yell out. Trini coughs and drops her fork on the floor.

"What's the matter with you? I could have choked, you stupid," Trini says.

Mickey gets up to put a hand over Trini's shoulder. "Maui, how rude," she says.

"No more games, Mickey," I say. "Something's up, and I won't take a bite out of this food until you tell me. So spill it, sis."

Trini reaches over for a bun and the butter and says, "Uhm, you're doing this hunger strike solo, bitch, I'm starving."

Mickey sighs. "Well," she says, pushing away her plate. "I was hoping we could've talked about it over ice cream, but since you insist, I'll get right to it."

The Mariposa Club

"Do," I say. I cross my arms.

"I'm going away to college," Mickey says, flatly.

My face lights up. "That's wonderful!" I say. "Oh, my God, Mickey, that's fantastic! Where are you off to? When?"

Mickey looks surprised by my reaction. I walk over to hug her and this seems to relax her. "Really? Oh, Maui, thank you! All week I've been dreading about telling you. I mean, I'll be done with my associate's degree at the end of this academic term, so this is the moment of truth: Am I going to a vocational school nearby or am I going to pursue my bachelor's? And I concluded, after plenty of back and forth that, my dream is to study law. And in order to get into a good law school, I need a strong undergraduate education. So, I plan to attend the University of California at Riverside and major in philosophy."

"You go, girl!" Trini shrieks. She walks up to hug Mickey as well. "I mean, all those cute college boys and an Olympic pool at the gym, where you can debrief to your heart's content! Whoohoo!"

"Well, that too," Mickey says, "but I imagine I'll be spending more time at the library."

"Mickey, I'm so proud of you," I say. "And Mami would've been so proud as well." We hug once more.

"Thank you for that, Maui," Mickey says. "That means a lot. God, I was so scared about telling you. I was afraid you would be upset."

"Upset?" I say. "Why would I? This is a wonderful opportunity for you."

"Well, you know, I thought that maybe you were planning to ditch this town to go off to college after you graduated from high school," Mickey says.

"Uh-oh," Trini blurts out. "I think this is the part of the drama where I take my plate into the other room." She picks up her food and makes a swift exit out of the dining area.

Rigoberto González

"I *am* planning to ditch this town to go off to college after graduation," I say. "I'm applying to universities even farther away from here than Riverside. I may even go off to another state."

Mickey shakes her head. "No, Maui," she says. "I stayed behind two years to take care of Papi. I could've run off as soon as I graduated high school too, but I didn't. I stayed here for him, and for you. Now it's your turn: you get to go to the local community college for a few years and *then* take off. We can't just cut ties with Papi and leave him here all alone. That would be awful! Plus, there's the money factor: Papi couldn't possibly put the two of us through college at the same time. And community college is way more inexpensive."

"I can't believe this!" I say, though something inside me tells me that this makes sense. That she's right: we can't just abandon our poor, widowed father, not after all the sacrifices he's made to make sure we are all right. But I also can't help feeling that this is unfair, that I'm being forced to accept an even bigger sacrifice— staying here, in boring old Caliente, California, when there's so much of the world left to explore.

"It's not about you believing it or not, Maui," she says. "It's about you accepting what has to be. Are you that selfish?"

"It's not about being selfish," I yell.

"Hey," she says. "Don't raise your voice at me."

"Sorry," I say. "But I think we need to talk about it a little more."

"What?" she says. "You just finished telling me how happy you are that I'm thinking about going off to college and now we have to talk about it a little more? What's to talk about? I'm either going or I'm not. And I'm *going*!"

"But-but-but, what about me?"

"What *about* you?" she says.

And I can't say it. It's sitting there with my brain throbbing as if a brick just dropped on top of it, but I can't say it. I will sound absolutely suck-ass selfish. *I* want to leave this town, *I* want to go away to college and let Mickey and Papi figure their lives out for themselves because *I* want to figure out *my* life. And I know my life isn't going to go anywhere sticking around here. What's there for a gay kid in Caliente? Nothing! It's not fair. It's absolutely not fair.

"I don't understand you, Maui," Mickey says, her voice softer this time. "Don't you love me? I'm your only sister who's looked after you all these years that Mami has been gone. Don't you love Papi? Here's a little challenge for you: grow up." And with that, she bolts out of the house.

Trini walks in with an empty plate in her hands and then points at my food with her fork. "So, are you going to eat that?" she asks.

My shoulders drop. "Oh, Trini, I'm just one big screw up. First I make you feel like shit and then I come home and make my sister feel like shit."

"That's why we call people like you *assholes*," Trini says.

I roll my eyes. "Nice."

Trini adds, "Well, I'll say this about la Mickey: it certainly is a surprising change of pace. I mean, I thought that girl was in college to get herself hitched, and then she turns around and decides she wants to be a lawyer. Wow. She either thinks she can look good in a skirt suit or else she hit her head, because I just can't see it."

I suddenly get defensive. "She's a smart girl, you know. She just doesn't like to show it."

"Well, in any case, this puts a damper on your plans as well. Looks like the only one who's going to ditch this dead club is Lib, who's still a junior anyway."

My eyes narrow. "You're enjoying this, aren't you?"

"What?" Trini says.

Rigoberto González

"You like the idea that Isaac and I will be stuck in this town just like you. Well, I've got news for you: I'm going off to college, no matter what. I've got the grades, I've got the smarts, and there's no way in hell I'm going to waste my days hanging around this dead-end street."

"Don't throw shade, missy, just because you weren't woman enough to throw it at your sister. *She's* the one you have to tell, not me. I cannot care less if you stay or go. Same with Isaac. Because I'll still be fierce me. And I've got plans too you know." Trini adjusts the silk collar on her blouse. "I plan to move up to Palm Springs and get a job at one of those night clubs, hosting drag shows and running bingo games after weekend brunch. I'm going to be fabulous, fierce, and famous!" She snaps her fingers after each of her *f*-words.

"You're joking," I say.

"No, I'm not," Trini says. "I'm going to be the hostess with the mostess, the lady of the lecherous and the glamorous, the top bitch, the desert's premier Diva deluxe."

Trini arches her back over the counter and pantomimes holding a cigarette.

"You mean Diva delusional," I say. "Who the hell are you, the Moses of 'mos? The sea of opportunity is going to part for your Mexican ass to simply come in and run the place?"

Trini's mouth drops. "Wow. Seems to me like you've got issues. And you know what else? I'm all out of tissues, so if you need to whine, weep, or bleed all over the place you can go ahead and let the meany mucus fester on your face 'cause I am so out of here, you're gonna need a radar to track my faggoty brown ass. You are one broken bitch that needs to put herself back together before anyone around here can look at you again. Right now, you're not just ugly, you're the *ugliest*."

With another snap of her fingers, Trini takes off to the bedroom. I'm left there standing in an empty kitchen with the food going cold, my limbs feeling shaky and getting a sudden case of claustrophobia. And to drive the final nail into this coffin that has locked its sides around me, Papi walks in through the front door.

"Good evening," he says in his cheerful voice. "Smells great. What's for dinner?"

"I can reheat you a plate if you want," I say, but don't wait for an answer. I simply do what I had seen my mother do many times when it was my father's turn to work late at the restaurant and her turn to get home early and cook for the family. After dinner, Mickey would rush over to her room to get on the phone with her friends. I'd sit at the table, watching Mami set aside a plate for my father and cover the food with the clear plastic wrap. The plate might sit there ten minutes, or a few hours, but eventually, once my father came home, it would travel from the counter to the microwave, from the microwave to the setting at the head of the table, where Papi waited anxiously to quell his hunger.

It once dawned on me that it was ironic that my father came home from a restaurant hungry, that it was odd how he didn't just step into the kitchen and ask for a plate of tacos or a bowl of soup—an order so simple, so quick, it would be no trouble at all. But after watching my parents sit together in the evenings, their voices lowered, except for the occasional burst of laughter or expression of surprise, I realized that this precious moment of intimacy is what kept my mother cooking, and my father coming home.

"How was work?" I ask my father after I stick the plate into the microwave. I turn around to watch him drop his body onto the chair.

"Fine," my father says. "Everything's just fine."

And I want to break down into tears right then and there, though I'm not sure what it is that I want to cry about. Am I sad for my poor father, the lonely man who will become lonelier still

Rigoberto González

after Mickey leaves home, after I do? Or am I sad for myself, the kid who wants to have a life outside of this dull, unexciting place, but who may have to stick around to walk its uneventful streets for a few years more?

The microwave dings, and I'm grateful that at least something around here can still have a song.

Goth Party

The next morning, Isaac, Trini and I march up to the principal's office to turn ourselves in. We sit in silence along the wall and this time the secretary gives us one of those looks with the raised eyebrows as she dials Boozely.

Principal Beasley comes out, combover and all, and appears more annoyed than upset.

"So," says the principal. "What's this I hear about an unauthorized leave from school grounds? You realize that we are responsible for you until the end of the final period? What if something terrible had happened? What were we supposed to tell your parents, huh?"

We don't answer because we're not supposed to. We're not even supposed to nod or shake our heads. This is the rule of high school discipline: sit there like a blank wall and let the pissed-off administrator spit-wad his anger at you until you can't take it anymore.

"I'm very, very surprised at you. One minute you waltz in here expecting me to approve your idea for a club, and the next you break one of the most important rules we have to protect your safety. Am I to trust your judgment after this?"

My face reddens. If Boozely nixes the Mariposa Club I'm not sure what's going to keep me from throttling Trini.

"What do you think, Mr. Dutton?"

God, I hate it when teachers do this, when they place the burden of wise thinking on the kid who messed up, just to show him that he was too stupid to distinguish right from wrong when it really mattered.

"We shouldn't have left school grounds without permission," Isaac mumbles.

"What's that? I didn't quite hear you?" says the principal, and now I have the urge to throttle him instead. Geez, let it go, already! Strike us down with a ruler and get it over with. I thought torture was illegal in *this* country.

"We shouldn't have left school grounds without permission," Isaac says, clearer this time.

I can hear Trini sighing, but we agreed not to bother with an explanation since, the fact is, we did break the rules. Besides, where do we begin? How do we tell this straight, funny-looking man with the dancing combover that this is your typical adolescent queer drama? ACT I: Girlfriend rushes off to the woods. ACT II: Girlfriend's girlfriends rush off after her. ACT III: Girlfriends hug and kiss and spend the afternoon redecorating.

Boozely turns his attention to me. "Well, Mr. Gutiérrez?"

I'm shaken awake. Now I've done it. I zoned out and totally missed what the principal just asked me.

"Yes, sir," I say, confidently.

"Yes, what?" the principal asks.

"Yes, to what you just said."

"And what did I just say?"

Rigoberto González

I surrender. "I'm not sure."

"Crash landing," Trini sing-songs. Isaac rolls his eyes.

"All right, look, I'm sick of this. I've got meetings to attend. I can't stay here playing games," the principal says. "I'll have Ms. López here write up your detention notices, which I expect you to bring back signed by your guardians on Monday, when you will serve your first day after school."

Isaac gasps. My body stiffens. All I can think of—and I'm sure Isaac's thinking the same thing—is about Mr. Dutton.

"How long's our detention?" I say.

"Three days."

"Three days?" Isaac says.

"And if I hear one word of objection, I'll make it four."

We sit there, speechless.

"And you're getting off easily, Mr. Gutiérrez," the principal says. "This offense usually warrants suspension. But since this is a first offense—and I hope the last—for all three of you, a simple three-day detention will do. Is that understood?"

"Yes, sir," we say in unison.

"Oh, Mr. Beasley, sir," I say, raising my hand like a dope.

"Mr. Gutiérrez?" the principal says.

"I do hope this won't hurt the request we made, about the club?"

"Well, it certainly didn't help," he answers. "That is a conversation for another occasion, and hopefully on one that is not as disappointing as this one."

I nod my head.

"Ms. López? Hall passes for these young men." And without a goodbye, the principal turns around and steps away to his private office. The secretary hands us our passes and ushers us out of the administration building.

"Three days!" Isaac says as soon as we're outside. "My father's going to kill me!"

The Mariposa Club

"Well, what if I explain it to him?" I suggest.

Isaac slides hands slowly over his face. "Don't worry about it," he says with resignation. "It won't help. Besides, you have your own father to deal with."

"Uh-oh," Trini says. "He's not going to be happy that we both got busted. He's not going to ground us, is he?"

"Yes, he's going to ground us," I say. "Damn! And tonight's the Goth party at Celie's."

"Well, we can tell him *after* the party, can't we? I mean, he won't even be home in time for us to tell him, otherwise we would," Trini says.

And I know it's wrong, and I know we shouldn't withhold information from our guardian to our selfish benefit, but I can see us diving into the wreck one more time, lapsing into the lack of judgment we call "teenager logic."

Guilt doesn't stop Trini and me from sifting through the closets looking for black clothing. Mickey's not much help because she never wears black. Besides, she's still upset with me and keeps her interactions to monosyllabic replies and silent shoulder-shrugs.

"Hey, can I wear this?" Trini says, holding up one of my mother's dresses.

I don't reply. I'm startled suddenly at the fact that we haven't tossed out any of Mami's old wardrobe, which looks horribly outdated. "I guess," I say, finally, and only because I can't remember my mother ever wearing it. Otherwise I'd feel kind of funny about it.

Trini has her own set of black boots, wig, and makeup, though she opts to wear red lipstick instead of black. She does, however, locate a deep magenta nail polish, which she uses on my fingers, and then on hers, and then on her toes.

Rigoberto González

"But you're wearing boots," I tell her. "Why paint your toe-nails?"

"You never know," Trini says.

Once we're dressed and painted, Trini combs my hair up into a stiff mohawk, using gobs of gel from a large crusty container we found in the bathroom closet. She weaves her wig into two Poca-hontas braids and keeps the entire thing in place with a black bandanna.

"We look ridiculous," I say.

"That's the Goth look," Trini says. "We'll fit right in."

Half an hour later, Isaac pulls up and honks his horn. Trini rushes out of the bathroom with my father's black shaving-kit travel bag clutched in her hand.

"Why are you bringing *that*?" I ask.

"It's my purse, silly," she says.

"Well, you better not lose it," I say, too anxious to get out of there before Papi gets home.

Isaac looks a little more dignified with his short blond hair slightly spiked and a simple black t-shirt advertising his father's jewelry store in Spanish: JOYERIA DUTTON.

"We live in the Southern California desert," he explains. "It's the only black shirt I have."

And we're off through the humid avenues to strike a pose at Reconcíliate García's Annual Goth Get-Together & Freak Show. Invitation only.

Celie's place is, well, Gothic. I remember the fra-cas she caused when she decided to paint her little house gray with dark purple trim. It was enough for the neighbors to put up with all the wrought-iron around the residence—fences, window guards, lawn sculptures that resembled back-in-the-day, back-in-the-old-country field weapons. Like the row of black metal spears that rise like a death threat, which is the first thing that stands out as soon as we drive up to the house. The second thing that catches the eye is that penis piñata, prominently set on the old-fashioned wrought-iron swinging porch bench. An older Goth dude in a black shiny vest and matching leather cap sits next to the penis, keeping it company. ("Two dicks," Trini says. "Get it?") Needless to say, Celie beat the complaint. In the end, the neighbors who didn't get used to it must have left the block eventually, since no gripe has landed her in court again.

Isaac parks behind a white hearse, which gets us all excited again. Skulls and skeletons are wired sporadically along the metal gates, and streamers of red run down the sills to suggest a bleeding wall. A white veil cascades down the only tree in the yard, making it look like a Godzilla bride. The strobe light pulsing inside shows through the windows and it's like lightning striking from within the house.

"Fierce!" Trini declares.

But the best surprise is yet to come.

Once we make our way past the welcome of bones, Bridezilla, the two dicks on the swinging bench, and a sea of glowing black velvet, white makeup, black lipstick, black lace, satin, fishnet stockings, corsets, leather bikinis, top hats, belts, frocks, and metal buttons on every ethnic group of Goth imaginable, we are stunned motionless when we come across Lib.

To borrow Lib's expression: Oh. My. Goddess.

It's not that there's anything particularly striking about his Goth gear, which is a crushed velvet cape over a basic black outfit. It isn't even the eyeliner, the porcupine spikes, and the lipstick. It's the confidence he exudes in his new appearance, a type of self-assurance and self-love that goes beyond the vain, self-absorbed big girl we have always known. He's surrounded by artificial smoke and a swirl of music that sounds part techno, part pulling the intestines out of a live cat.

Rigoberto González

"Will you look at that?" Trini says, clearly as impressed as I am.

"She's in her element," Isaac says. It's true. And suddenly I realize that this is more than a Goth party—this is Lib's debutante ball. Lib has arrived.

"Good evening, girls!" Lib yells out as he walks toward us. The techno-heavy music grows louder.

"Hey!" I say. Trini goes up to Lib and gives him the up-and-down.

"Good Goth!" Trini says.

"Celie helped out!" Lib says.

"I can hardly hear you!" I say.

Lib shakes his head. "Never mind! Just have a good time!"

In exchange for entry into the wildest party in Caliente, California, none of us high school students are allowed to drink alcohol or smoke pot. Celie, in her gorgeous diaphanous gown and felt hat crowned with black roses, walks around as if she's still running security over at the Lame View Mall and keeps an eye on everything. Though I can't imagine she has to do the same level of watch-dogging over Snake or Maddy, who are both eighteen, but still not old enough to drink, but not interested in anything else at the moment but each other. Yes, we Fierce Foursome are not the only high school students in attendance. It makes sense that Celie would invite Maddy, her former babysitting charge, and that Maddy in turn would bring along her new boyfriend, Snake.

Isaac elbows me when we come across the pair making out in matching old school heavy-metal band t-shirts on the living room couch.

"I know," I say.

"Hey!" Trini says. And when Maddy and Snake look up, Trini follows up with: "So how long have you two been screwing?"

"Trini!" Lib says.

The Mariposa Club

Maddy rolls her eyes and goes back to her liplock with Snake, and when we're too slow to leave, they both raise their middle fingers up at us without bothering to halt their kissing.

"Well!" Trini says. She flicks her braids and goes off into the crowd of partiers.

"Come with me upstairs!" Lib says. And we follow through the stench of clove cigarettes, cigars, pot, and some strange incense that's dispersed into the air in a useless attempt to cover up the other odors.

We enter one of the bedrooms on the second floor and close the door behind us, which muffles the music enough for us to hear each other's voices.

"Raging, isn't it?" Lib says.

"To say the least," Isaac says.

"You look fabulous, Lib!" I say. "I like it."

Lib strikes a pose. "It's the new me. Who knew? All this time watching Celie parade around in black and then suddenly I find my way. Now we are two Goth girls in the family."

"Well, at least it'll be familiar territory for your parents," Isaac says.

"Totally," says Lib. "Hey, so I found out who's doing detention duty this coming week. I overheard them talking about it at the administration office."

"You little eavesdropper, you," I say. "Who?"

"Ms. Disaster."

I laugh. "You're kidding me! Oh, man, it's going to be a piece of cake."

"No doubt," Isaac says, but without conviction.

"You okay, Isaac?" I say. "How did things work out with your father?"

"How did things work out with yours?" he retorts.

"Truce," I say. "Let's change the subject."

"Agreed," Isaac says.

Rigoberto González

We sit in silence, regarding one another for a few seconds until the door bursts open and a pair of young Goths tumbles in with their arms around each other. One of them has his face buried in the other's pale neck.

"Oops," the one getting his neck sucked says. "Sorry, girls, we thought this bedroom was vacant."

"So, where should I bleed you dry, baby?" the neck-sucker asks him.

"Let's try the attic," the one getting his neck sucked says. "Celie calls it 'The Catacombs,' because it's cobwebby, drafty, and damp."

"Shouldn't the catacombs be underground?" the neck-sucker asks.

"Who gives a bat's ass?" the other says.

"Up to the catacombs, then," the neck-sucker yells. He turns to us and says, "Carry on, girls," before they tumble back out without separating as he shuts the door.

"All righty, then," Isaac says.

"Oh. My. Goth. That was hot," Lib swoons. "Maybe they'll let us watch."

"Sure," I say, rolling my eyes, though that's only to hide the fact that I'd *love* to watch, and that I just got aroused enough to warrant crossing my legs.

"Okay, Goth gals," Lib says. "I do have one little surprise for you."

"Hmmm..." I say. "I was wondering why you dragged us up here. Pun intended."

Lib starts to giggle. "Oh. My. Goth. I'm giddy with delight," he manages to say.

"Spill it, Lib," Isaac says. "You're freaking me out."

"Okay, okay." He takes a deep breath and takes turns looking at us. "I'm graduating with you guys."

"What?" Isaac and I ask in unison. "What do you mean? That you're a senior now? Since when?" I add.

"I will be. Next semester," Lib says. "Once I take the advanced placement exams, which will be like eating pudding. You know I always test off the charts on those things. I mean, I'm already a National Merit Scholar."

"Wait," Isaac says. "You're taking the APs? You just took the PSAT last year."

"And when I kicked ass, I got a special invitation to the National Merit Scholarship Competition. The results came in a week ago, but we've all been a little *distracted*."

"So, wait," I say. "Why the hell do you want to graduate early? Why do you want to do your senior year in one semester? Why do you want to put yourself out in the real world this soon?"

"Because then we get to stay together," Lib says. "The three of us anyway since Trini couldn't even get into a cosmetology school with her rock bottom transcript. And did you get a good look at her hair? It's a Goth party, not a pow-wow."

"What do you mean, 'stay together'?" Isaac asks.

"You know, we get to be the Fierce Threesome. In college, wherever we choose to go. I'm partial to anything in San Francisco or maybe New York. Wouldn't it be fierce? The three of us going away to school together and being roomies and everything. Oh, my Goth, it's going to be great!"

Stillness descends in the room even though I can still hear the music pulsing through the walls of the house. Someone scampers down the hall outside the door, perhaps the two Goth queens who finished enjoying whatever it is two Goth queens do in cobwebby, drafty, and damp attic catacombs at a house party on a Friday night. And they will probably enjoy it some more as they take their intimate two-person sub-party to another location, maybe someplace cobwebbier, draftier, and damper.

Rigoberto González

"Why the grim faces, girls?" Lib says. "Does it bother you that I'm a senior now?"

"No, Lib," I say. "Not at all. I'm happy for you. I'm happy for all of us."

"Me, too," Isaac says in a flat tone.

"Group hug!" Lib announces, and we rise to collect our bodies into one.

A knock at the door breaks the spell. "Yoo-hoo!" Trini calls out, and then she opens the door. When she sees us standing there with our arms around each other, she says in her fake southern belle speak: "What are y'all doin'? Squeezin' the silicone out of Lib's titties?"

"Too late for that," Lib retorts. "When you walked in, your face evaporated the filling out of them."

Besides that brief exchange of cattiness between Lib and Trini, the rest of the evening goes by without incident, though Lib doesn't appreciate how unimpressed Trini is with his big plans. By ten o'clock, Celie comes around to kick us out of the party.

"Bedtime, kids," she tells us. And then she wipes the grin off of Lib's face when she adds: "You too, Goth squirt."

"I'm dying in these heels, anyway," Trini says. "Get me to my bunny slippers!"

We pass the gate where two tough Goth guys stand guard. They let us out with a nod and block a few members of Los Calis from getting in.

"Come on, man, we've got the goods and shit," Tony Sánchez says. He's the member of the group still in high school. He's not allowed to drop out because the gang needs him to supply the high school potheads. He waves a bag of pot in the Goth bouncer's face.

"Not your party, dude," the Goth bouncer replies.

"How about you kids? You need anything?" one of the other guys says to us.

The Mariposa Club

"We're good," Isaac says.

"I know those guys," Tony says. "They smoke the *other* way, if you know what I mean." His buddies laugh along with him. Tony watches us walk to the car. I feel particularly uneasy and singled out because he locks eyes with me.

As soon as we're in the car, Lib says, "Is it my imagination or did my gaydar go off with that Tony Sánchez?"

"Closet case," Trini says in a sing-song voice.

"Yeah, well," I say. "It's going to stay that way, so don't even go knocking."

Isaac drops Trini and me off first, and then turns the car around to head to the south side to Lib's place, but he's slow to get going. The Honda stalls at the street.

"What's wrong?" I ask, turning back. Isaac simply stares at me, as if he wants to tell me something, but he only sits there frozen. "Are you okay, Isaac?"

Isaac smiles weakly, makes a sad attempt at a wave, and drives off.

Strange. I will have to ask him about it at the Latino banquet tomorrow. Trini and I step into the house, where my father, unfortunately, sits in front of the TV in the living room. We have no choice but to be seen.

"Hey, Papi," I say as casually as I can.

"Hey, Mr. Gutiérrez," Trini says.

Papi sits up. "My goodness! Halloween already?"

"It was a Goth party at Celie's, Lib's sister," Trini explains.

"What in the world is a Goth?" Papi asks.

"A Goth is—" Trini begins, but I interrupt.

"Papi, we have something to tell you."

"Oh," Papi says. "Not too serious, I hope. Sit."

Trini and I take our places next to Papi on the couch, and then I tell the whole sordid tale about my fight with Trini: Trini's unauthorized leave from the school grounds, then Isaac's and mine,

Rigoberto González

our pending afterschool detention, and our convenient flight to the Goth party before he got home from work in order to avoid getting grounded and missing it altogether.

It's this last admission that annoys Trini, who glares at me with disbelief that I would just sing like a canary on speed. It's also what upsets my father the most.

"I can forgive everything, except trying to get away with something," Papi says. "Maui, I'm surprised at you, disappointed. And Trini, I think it's safe to say that you know better as well. So, your punishment will carry over past detention. As soon as you're done there, you are to report to the restaurant for kitchen duty."

"You mean, death by dishpan hands?" Trini shrieks.

My father furrows his brow.

"Never mind, Papi," I say. "Yes, we accept the penalty." I elbow Trini.

"Ye-yes," she stutters. "What Maui said."

"Good. Now get a good night's sleep because tomorrow we have the Latino Chamber of Commerce banquet. And don't forget: costumes. But not the ones you're wearing now. That just doesn't quite fit the evening's theme."

"I am beat," Trini says. "I'm not sure I'll be able to pull another long day in heels."

"Oh, about that," I say. "Trini, let me break something to you about what you're going to wear tomorrow." I put my arm over Trini's shoulder as we walk into the bedroom.

The Latino Banquet

We don't have to wake up early since our stint at Las Cazuelas is a late-in-the-day engagement, but my eyes still open wide at seven a.m.—my usual wake-up time on a school day. We still haven't brought the extra bed in from the shed, which means Trini and I have been sleeping together this whole week. Truth is it doesn't bother me. Since we're like sisters, nothing sneaky or freaky happens beneath the sheets, even when Trini rolls around all night and drops her heavy hand over my face. She may be on the small side but she carries a mean punch.

I suppose this is a good a time as any to reflect on everything that's happened this week, which seems unreasonably burdened with drama, but then again, this *is* adolescence, this *is* high school senior year, this *is* four young queens trying to find our footing in the shaky world.

When my mother died, I was on the verge of thirteen, which she called "hurteen" because it's still the middle of the ugly stage—puberty, zits, body hair, body odor, hormones, hormones, and more hormones. No matter what mirror you look at you still see the awkward overgrown child trying to sharpen his angles and hide his baby fat in order to fool himself into thinking he's one step closer to attractive.

My own body was soft in all the wrong places and narrow in a few strange ones, like that section of my torso between my ribs and my hips. It gave me a wasp-like appearance that forced me to wear extra-large t-shirts during my freshman year of high school. I imagine Isaac's the only one of the four of us who was pretty from the get-go. He was probably born with broad shoulders, narrow hips, and flawless skin. His only visible defect is that he burns easily in the sun. Wow. Where can we find him a support group?

In any case, it seemed so simple back then to worry about a pimple on the nose, an involuntary hard-on at the end of art class, just as the bell was about to ring for lunch.

I can't help but think that if my mother were alive I'd be in much better shape. I wouldn't have to worry about giving up on my dream of going away to college, or about being queer around the house. I'm certain she would let me keep my Vin Diesel and Daniel Craig posters up on the wall. And she would march down to Principal Beasley's office herself to demand that the school support the Mariposa Club.

But my mother isn't here. Her name, Adelita, as in the women soldiers of the Mexican Revolution, a memory, a ghost of the past much like her namesakes.

Trini lets out a fart. I roll my eyes in her direction. She blinks a few times before she sees me. Stretching in bed she asks, "What time is it?"

"Time for an emergency evacuation," I say. "Phew! Death by poison gas!"

"We call it 'the vapors,'" Trini says, indignant. "And it's rather unladylike for you to point it out. Don't you have any manners?

Rigoberto González

Do you see *me* pinching my nose at the assault of *your* baboon breath? What have you been eating: freckled banana peel with bugs on top?"

"Damn, you're bitchy in the morning," I say.

"Forgive me, Passion Flower," Trini says. "I had a horrible nightmare."

"About?"

"I dreamed that I was a kitchen slave, just like Cinderella, except that the little rodents didn't come to dress me in silk and the little shits with wings didn't swoop down to tie ribbons on my hair. I was gnawed and pecked and pecked and gnawed until I looked like one of those green zombies on that old Michael Jackson music video. Or maybe worse—I *was* Michael Jackson, all tore up and feeling the floor to find my nose."

Trini puts her fingers on her face for effect. "And then," she continues, "there was mariachi music and it wouldn't stop even though my ears were bleeding. And my mean old stepsister—we'll call her Mauina—she stomps in to demand that I make enchiladas from scratch. 'Oh, oh, certainly, big sister boss, but please, no more tortilla-slaps!' And so then—"

"I'll show you a tortilla slap, you anal thermometer!" I say, as I lift my head up to pull my pillow out in order to whack her.

"Truce! Truce!" she calls out, but I show no mercy. Silly girls get silly how-do-you-do's on the side of their silly ol' heads.

Once we're done whacking each other with pillows, we simply lie there looking up at the ceiling.

"What did you used to have up there?" Trini asks.

"What?" I say, but I know what she's talking about. "When I was younger, Mami stuck glow-in-the-dark stars up there. I pretended I was sleeping outdoors. And each of those stars was a guardian angel that watched over me."

"So why did you take them down?"

The Mariposa Club

"I don't know," I say, though I know the answer to this also: it was my loss of faith after my mother died. I used a broom handle to knock the stickers down, but not before leaving behind some scrapes and dents on the ceiling.

"I wish I still had my mother," Trini says. "I miss her. We used to be such girlfriends. We used to watch Mexican soaps on TV and giggle at the love scenes. We'd go to the clothing stores and try on fancy coats we couldn't afford. We made the perfect mother-daughter tag team. And suddenly it came to a close, like the end of a feel-good movie, the credits rolling nothing but reminders that it was all make-believe."

I'm about to ask, "And then what happened?" But I know: Little Trini grew up, and that shamed her parents because Big Trini walks out the door and into the open, into the line of sight of the neighbors.

"It's so sad, isn't it?" Trini says. "That people should care that much about how we're so different from everyone else. I wonder why that bothers them?"

"Maybe," I say. "It's because they see themselves in us."

"Or maybe," Trini says. "It's because they don't."

We keep staring up at the chips and dents and scrapes on the ceiling. They're more true to life than the artificial decorations of those glow-in-the-dark stars: plenty of wear and tear, but still holding on.

At four o'clock that afternoon, while I finish up some math and science homework—nothing I couldn't do in my sleep, except that I prefer to sleep while I sleep—Mickey knocks on the bedroom door and peeks in. Trini's lying on her stomach on the bed, catching up on some reading for her remedial English class. Somehow she's been getting inspired to do some homework of her own, which goes against her convictions. I don't tease her about it because I want to encourage her to keep it up. In the background, I've got the Pet Shop Boys stimulating my brain cells.

"Ready to go to Las Cazuelas, kids?" Mickey asks.

"Already?" Trini says. "But I'm so absorbed reading this story set in some country that has nothing to do with my life: past, present, or future. Must I tear my eyes away now?"

"I'm sure the book will still be here when you return," Mickey says.

"Meow!" Trini retorts.

"Trini, stop," I say. And then I turn to Mickey. "Hey, Mickey can I talk to you for a second?"

Mickey rolls her eyes. "Sure. But make it quick. I have a study group to drive clear across town."

I rush up and pull her into the hall, closing the bedroom door behind us for privacy.

"Listen," I tell her. "I've been thinking about what you said. You know, about me sticking around to keep Papi company?"

"And?" Mickey says, sounding as if she's anticipating an argument.

"And, I think you're right. I *should* stay, that way he won't be alone. Not too alone, at least." I say this last sentence with my head down.

Mickey's face lights up. She wraps her arms around me and says, "Oh, Maui, thank you, thank you. I knew I could count on you. And don't worry, it's not forever. Just for a year or two, until Papi gets used to me being gone."

Just a year or two. As a seventeen-year-old, that sounds like an eternity to me, and suddenly the weight of my sister's body on mine makes me feel like I have just taken on her burdens, as if this hug signals the transfer of something unshakeable. Herpes, maybe. *Just a year or two.* Might as well say, just a finger or two. I'm only asking you to give up a few fingers. Here's the chopping block. Here's the axe. Now, dear madame, set your hand along the bloodied edge.

My body grows cold, as if my soul has taken a step back without taking the flesh along. What did I just do? What dotted line did I just sign?

Las Cazuelas is a stereotype of a restaurant—garish red and green colors, piñatas and wagon wheels, mariachi music, and lovely señoritas in white skirts and embroidered blouses. Saturdays it's the margarita special and two-for-one tacos, lunchtime buffets, and the guacamole cart. The banquet room is in the back and tonight only Trini, Lib, Isaac, and I get to flutter around from table to table, filling water pitchers and removing empty plates. We're not servers, just extra help while the regular workers take care of the clientele on the main floor.

I'm not really embarrassed by the touristy nature of the place, just a little confused since most of the population in Caliente, California is Mexican, Mexican-American, or Chicano. Maybe it's some nostalgic thing—middle-class people's need for refried beans and tortillas, the staples of the working class.

Mickey's mood has changed, so she lets me plug in her iPod with its mix of Cyndi Lauper, old Madonna (her recent stuff sucks!), old Britney (her recent stuff also sucks!), and new Christina, and then a couple of hip-hop selections—Beyoncé and Mary J.—just to give us some street cred. I like women singers mostly, I guess because I like to lip-synch to the lyrics, making believe that it's me up there shaking my hair extensions.

"Do you see Isaac's car anywhere?" Trini asks, scoping out the parking lot as we drive in.

"Can't tell," I say. "This place is hopping tonight."

"So don't cause trouble, you two," Mickey says. "This is a business, not a playground. I'll pick you guys up at the end of my study group. Call me, but don't expect me to get here in five minutes. Just be patient; I'll get here."

"Not to worry, girlfriend," Trini says. "We're going to keep it real tonight, here in Little Mexico."

"I mean it," Mickey adds. "Tonight's an important banquet night. Very influential people will be dining here and Papi wants to make a good impression."

Thankfully, we drive up to the entrance and I don't have to hear any more preaching from Sister Micaela. *What* is her problem? I mean, we're getting paid and everything. This is a job, not a favor.

"See you later!" I yell out as I wave. Trini stands next to me with a duffle bag. "Why did you bring that for?" I ask.

"A change of clothes," Trini says. "One never knows."

"Well, our costumes are waiting for us inside," I say. "Dibs on the outfit from Veracruz."

Entering Las Cazuelas is dramatically different from our entrance to the Goth party the night before. Here it's all fiesta and Mexican flag streamers and trumpets that blare out across the scent of red sauce and melted American cheese. Waiters smile as they balance the trays of empty plates and margarita glasses with only a few smears of salt still clinging to the rims.

"Good evening, Mauricio," Yolanda, the hostess, says as soon as she sees me. She greets everyone because she's the prettiest girl on staff. Her dark thick hair contrasts nicely with the deep red lipstick, and she might as well be one of those Aztec goddesses depicted on the calendar the restaurant gives out during Christmas season.

"This is Trini," I tell her.

"Hello, gorgeous," Trini says.

"Hello, to you too," Yolanda says, never relaxing her smile. "Mr. Gutiérrez is in the back room."

The Mariposa Club

"Hey, have Isaac or Lib shown up yet?" I ask. "They're my two friends also working the banquet room tonight."

Yolanda shakes her head. "No, not yet."

Trini and I head to the back. I make a mental note to call Isaac's cell if he doesn't show up within the next thirty minutes, though I can't imagine Isaac flaking out or changing his plans without letting me know.

The back room is both the changing room and the staff room. The lockers don't have locks because no one really keeps any valuables here and the closet in the corner is reserved for the Mexican costumes. Back in the heyday, when my mom ran the place, Las Cazuelas used to have ballet folklórico shows on the weekends. I remember being dazzled by the colorful skirts on the female dancers, and being charmed by the tight mariachi pants that tapered down the legs of the male dancers, a vertical row of silver buttons dropping to the slim ankles. The group my mom hired was a Mexican dance club from Mickey's community college, but it eventually disbanded and the restaurant ended up inheriting the costumes because they had been stored here all along and no one from the troupe ever came back to claim them.

And they've hung there ever since, getting dusted whenever the banquet hall is in use and the manager wants to give the night's special event an extra bit of ethnic flair.

"Look at these dresses!" Trini yells out. "They're fabulous!"

"Remember what I told you, Trini," I say. "This is a more conservative affair, so we can only use the men's costumes. It'll be fine. Here, this is a colorful one."

I pull out a green, flowery shirt worn for the dance numbers from Nayarit and Guerrero—two very different states, but with similar aggressive stomping. I suppose the colorful shirt tones down the heavy masculinity some. On Trini, it'll erase it completely.

Rigoberto González

"Bo-ring," Trini sings as he unfurls the matching flowery dress worn by the women. "Oh, my God, are these fake braids?"

Indeed, the braids that the women clip on and off as they change in and out of their regional costumes are dangling from a tie rack. Each woman has a few pairs because the ribbons braided into the hair have to match the color of the costume. Trini clips on a pair with blue ribbon.

"Ajúa!" she says.

I take out a white guayabera with a red scarf sticking out of the pocket. I remember watching the men wrap the scarves around their necks and how they held them in place by sliding the ends through a ring until the ring reached the base of their Adam's apples. It was such a sexy gesture. I'd sit nearby, quietly observing, pretending I was just fascinated by the transformations into folk dancers from Veracruz but all the while I sat there fantasizing about encounters with these lean, muscled bodies.

"You got a ring I can borrow?" I ask Trini.

"Will my toe ring do? What do you need one for?"

"Uhm, never mind," I say.

After a bit of compromise, Trini opts for the white pants from the Veracruz costume, the flowery shirt from Nayarit, and the black coat with silver buttons from the mariachi outfit—from the state of Jalisco, if you really need to know. I keep it simple: the guayabera and black slacks. I suppose the mix and match won't bother anyone if we're only there to refill water glasses and bread baskets.

I'm just about to mention that Isaac and Lib are late when Lib comes rushing in through the door.

"Hey, I made it," he says. He's dressed completely in black, his fingernails are still painted, and he's wearing eyeliner.

"What the hell?" I say. "You didn't have time to change since last night? And where's Isaac?"

"Isaac, I'll have you know, never came to pick me up. I even called him like five times on the cell and it was off the whole time, so I had Papi drop me off on his way to the soup kitchen," Lib says, catching his breath. "And, *this*—" he takes a dramatic stance by throwing his shoulders back and posing—"is who I am. Learn it. Live it. Love it. Even my own father has to learn to deal with it."

"Well, look at *her*," Trini says. "One night at the Goth party and she's Elvira, Mistress of the Dark. Lose your bat, honey?"

"Wait a minute, wait a minute," I say. "What do you mean Isaac wouldn't answer your calls?"

At this point one of the young Mexican waiters comes in wearing street clothes, ready to change into his uniform for his shift. He stops in his tracks when he sees us standing there like displaced circus performers.

"Orale," he says.

"Orale," someone replies, but I'm not sure if it's me, Lib, or Trini because we're all stunned ourselves at how handsome this guy is. We stop breathing when his shirt comes off. Only a few years older than us, he's got the dark tan of someone who also works in the agricultural fields harvested in the Caliente Valley—grape, onion, asparagus, lettuce. His hair is curly and pitch black. His torso is slim and his back muscled and well-defined. He moves forward with his own costume change, most likely self-conscious as he stands there with his shirt off and as we stand there gawking—three sets of hungry eyes. The interlude lasts no more than a few minutes since he bolts out as soon as he's able to.

"Do you think he'd mind if we sniff his street clothes?" Lib says.

"Girl, I can still sniff his underclothes," Trini says. "That's like imprinted on my brain. Did you take a good look at his shoulders?"

Rigoberto González

"Oh, I know," I say, not able to resist, but then I shake it off. "Hey, wait a minute! Facts first, fantasy second. Where the hell's Isaac?"

Lib shakes his head. "I told you, I don't know," he says. "He never came to pick me up. He should be showing up soon, I mean, it's not like him to flake out. Maybe there's been a family emergency or something. Maybe you should try calling his father at the jewelry store?"

"Good idea," I say. "Okay, listen, we're running late here. We're supposed to be *in* the dining hall at five o'clock. That's ten minutes from now. So Lib: take the makeup off and get yourself into one of these babies. Then join Trini as soon as you can. Trini: Hold fort at the banquet room. Tell Papi I'll be there as soon as I find out what's the deal with Isaac."

"Don't worry," Trini says. "Everything will be under control."

I don't like the subtle yet noticeable sneaky tone in Trini's voice but I have no time to argue. I rush out to the manager's office to make a phone call. On the way there I see Papi walking swiftly out of the banquet room, but before I have a chance to wave or call out to him, he's stopped by a gray-haired gentleman dressed in a conservative three-piece suit and it looks like the conversation is serious so I decide not to interrupt.

The manager's office is always unlocked. I remember Mickey and me having to do homework here many afterschool afternoons, and years later, it was Maddy and me when Mickey wasn't available for babysitting duties. The large desk gets great light from the window right behind it, which faces the as-of-yet undeveloped desert. And for a moment I have this vision of Mami sitting behind it as she turns the pages of a ledger.

But I don't have time for a strut down memory lane. I quickly sit on the chair and dial the jewelry store at Lame View Mall.

"Joyería Dutton," Mr. Dutton says. "We'll be closing in five minutes."

The Mariposa Club

"Mr. Dutton, it's Mauricio," I say.

"Mauricio, I was hoping you would call. Is Isaac with you?"

The question gives me chills.

"I'm afraid not, Mr. Dutton, that's why I'm calling you," I say. My voice trembles a bit. "I was hoping you could tell me. He was supposed to meet me at my father's restaurant half an hour ago but he's not here."

"Oh, Isaac..." Mr. Dutton says, and then his voice grows faint as he mumbles something in Irish or Scottish or Welsh—I never quite took note of Isaac's exact family heritage. All I know is that when Isaac's father gets lost in his native language, it's not good.

"Mr. Dutton?" I say. "Mr. Dutton?"

I can still hear him mumbling, as if he has placed the receiver on the display case and my voice is now directed at the shiny, but apathetic metals. I hang up.

Isaac, Isaac, what in the world are you up to? I know it's useless to try to reach him on the cell, but I wouldn't be a friend if I didn't try. I dial and immediately his voicemail picks up: *Hey, this is Isaac, leave a message and I'll get right back to you.*

Indeed. Suddenly I flash back to last night, to that odd look he gave me before he took off after dropping us off. I *knew* there was something suspicious.

"Isaac, it's Maui," I say. "Give me a call at Las Cazuelas and let me know what's going on. Trini and Lib are here. We'll be done by nine. I hope to hear from you by then. Love you."

Suddenly the celebratory music coming in over the speakers sounds obnoxious. In an instant, the smell of cheese and beans and tomato sauce repulses me. I think I'm going to be sick.

"Maui," Papi says. I'm so distracted I don't even notice when he opens the office door and sticks his head in.

"Papi! I'm sorry. I'm ready," I say, rushing out of my seat.

"I hope so," Papi says. "We have a little bit of a problem with your friends."

Rigoberto González

"Problem?" I say, and I really don't want to imagine what.

When we step into the banquet room, I come across different layers of outrage. The gray-haired gentleman dressed in a conservative three-piece suit is pissed that Trini's in drag and Lib's wearing makeup. Trini, wearing a pair of thick braids with orange ribbons, is pissed that the shoulders on her colorful Jalisco dress are a bit too wide for her frame and she looks like she's wearing sagging shoulder pads. Lib is pissed that there wasn't enough black in the costume closet so he pulled out a black table cloth from the linen closet and draped it over himself like a cape. Mr. Benson, the owner of the restaurant, is pissed because his manager, my father, is responsible for recruiting the extra help and they turn out to be freaks. Papi is pissed because the owner and the gray-haired gentleman dressed in a conservative three-piece suit called my friends freaks, and because he trusted me to inform my friends that there's a time and a place for everything and that for cross-dressing and going-Goth, the Latino Chamber of Commerce Annual Fundraising Banquet at Las Cazuelas is neither the time or the place. And I'm pissed that everybody's so self-involved that nobody except me is preoccupied with Isaac's whereabouts!

"This is outrageous! This is insulting! What kind of zoo are you running here?" the gray-haired gentleman says.

"Please, sir, please," Mr. Benson says. "We beg your pardon." He then turns to my father: "Gutiérrez?"

"Maui, take your friends outside," Papi says apologetically.

"Does this mean we're not getting paid?" Trini says. She insists on keeping the dress fanned open, her hands holding it up so that she looks like a sunrise.

The gray-haired gentleman and Mr. Benson turn their backs and whisper while my father looks on, looking distressed.

The handsome young Mexican waiter who earlier changed in front of us comes by with a platter of empties balanced on a tray. "Orale!" he says, his eyes fixed on the ruckus as he steps in and out of view.

"Let's go change guys," I say with very little conviction in my voice. And I'm hoping that when we step into our street clothes again, everything that happened while we were wearing these costumes will also get lifted off my shoulders.

Rigoberto González

Where's Isaac?

"You know, I've had an insight," Trini says. She and I are sitting in the back seat of Mr. García's car. Lib sits in the front, dozing, his head pressed against the seat because it's been an exhausting night. After getting canned from the function at Las Cazuelas on the spot, we had to wait around for the first possible ride. In this case not Celie or Isaac or Mickey, but dependable Mr. García, Lib's father, but only after he got back from some tent revival down by the Mexican border, two hours away.

"Do I really want to know?" I say. I'm grateful at least that Papi didn't get canned. We'll also have to do our detention penance elsewhere since it's clear Trini and I won't be welcomed back to Las Cazuelas anytime soon, even if we do show up to wash the dishes for free.

Trini taps her fingertip against her cheek. "The longer I live, the more I'm convinced that it's everybody else who's a drama queen, not me."

The comment is meant to elicit a laugh, maybe even a girlish titter. Ha ha, the world is *full* of drama queens! But that's not what happens. I'm sitting in the back seat of a car next to Trini. A few days ago I was sitting in the back seat of a car next to Trini. And I suspect, if I don't change something soon, if I don't do something different, that next week, and next month, and next year I will be sitting in the back seat of a car next to Trini. Static, stagnant, stationary Trini—she who is doomed to stay locked inside the Caliente Valley because she's got no way out. But I do. And yet I too will stay locked inside with her if I don't simply pick up and leave. Is that what Isaac did? I like to believe so. Maybe he's had it with his father and our high school and the Lame View Mall and with Lib and Trini and me, Maui, the kid who needs to grow some nuts and tell his big sister, *No! No, Mickey, I'm not sticking around this tired-ass town one second longer than I have to. I too am going away to college, to my freedom, my future.*

"Mars to Maui, Mars to Maui," Trini says.

"Shut up." I say.

"Excuse me?" Trini says, surprised that I'm upset with her for the tenth time this week.

"Just shut up, Trinidad Ramos," I say. "I hate you."

All of a sudden the car jerks to stop and that sends Trini and me flying into the seats in front of us.

"What the hay, Papi!" Lib says. "I was asleep!"

"Mauricio Gutiérrez, did I just hear you use the *h*-word?" Mr. García's eyes are looking at me through the rearview mirror as alarming as headlights.

"The *h*-word?" Lib says. "Homo?"

"No, you zippity doo Goth," Trini says. "Maui just admitted that he hates me. Hate hate hate! He's a hater, hater masturbator."

"Trinidad, for the love of God," Mr. García says.

"Hater, hater, viper-gator!"

"Maui, what the hay is this about?" Lib says.

Rigoberto González

And now I'm annoyed at Lib with his "hay this" and "hay that."

"Say 'hell,' you raccoon face," I yell. "Better yet say it like you mean it: hell, hell, hell! 'What the *hell* is this about?'"

"Maui, don't disrespect my father. I would never curse like that in front of yours," Lib says.

"Oh, screw you, Lib," I say. "You just almost got my father fired, showing up in your vampire get-up. And you too, you second-hand-store drag queen. Why can't it be one of you who disappears? Better yet both of you go away. Why does it have to be Isaac? He should be here. Isaac's my friend. You two are selfish and self-centered and even put together you're nothing compared to Isaac! I hate *both* of you!"

"Mauricio, please," Mr. García says. "Enough of this language. Enough of this hate."

"Hate hate, defecate! Hate hate, defecate!" Trini chants.

"Trini, cut it out!" Lib says.

"Trinidad!"

"Hate hate, defecate!"

"Cut it out!"

"Please."

"Hate hate!"

"Cut it out!" Lib says again but all I can hear is: *Out! Out! Out!*

And the next thing I know I'm out. Running.

In the Caliente Valley there are still many untouched acres of desert and we happen to be pulled over next to one so that it feels like I'm doing one of those undocumented border crossings as my feet keep sinking into the soft sand. The further in I go the darker it becomes and the patches of desert brush begin to look like holes on the ground so I move around them, zigzagging now toward the void. I can hear Mr. García panting behind me, but I don't want him to catch me. I'm so ashamed about what I've said, which I didn't mean. I'm so ashamed I acted like an asshole

The Mariposa Club

in front of this good man and my best friends. The sweat begins to pour down my head, the tears down my face and suddenly I curse this impulsive choice to run toward the open desert and not toward the traffic or even toward the one highway bridge that has seen its share of jumpers over the years.

Is that what I want to do? Die? Metaphorically, anyway. Since this month has been chipping away at my life each day and today is the final blow. I'm as close to lifeless as I've ever been. That's what I feel like, a pile of broken stones, and my collapse has done nothing but lift dust.

September, September, all the beautiful things go away in September. My mother. Isaac. My dreams. All of these are my September sadnesses.

"Mauricio!" Mr. García calls out. He has stopped running, unable to keep up the chase. So I too stop to rest, to vomit with exhaustion. And then more comes out. I howl as if this sprint into the desert has turned me into a coyote. I imagine the real coyotes turning their snouts this way, alarmed by the grief released into the air.

"Mauricio," Mr. García says, softer this time because he's standing right beside me. He places his palm over my back and the touch reminds me that I'm human, and like the baby that I still am I break out into a fit of sobbing.

"I'm so sorry," I say, barely able to get the words out through my heaving and my dry mouth.

"It's okay, son," Mr. García says. "Everything's going to be fine."

"I don't know what's happening to me," I say between sobs. "I don't understand anything."

"Shh," Mr. García says. "Just breathe, Mauricio, you're hurting yourself. Let the silence soothe you. Let the air fill up your lungs. Everything's going to be fine."

Rigoberto González

I keep my back bent, my face to the ground. I let Mr. García comfort me. That's all I need for the moment: a sympathetic lie. I turn toward the side of the road. Lib and Trini sit inside the car with their hands pressed to the windows, their wide-eyed faces look pushed in and suffocated. Let them out, I say. Let my beautiful friends go.

No message from Isaac awaits me back home. It's confirmed: he's missing. This new crisis completely swallows up the Latino banquet fiasco so Papi avoids the subject altogether when he finally gets home. I'm in bed with my clothes still on, curled up with my arms around a pillow. The door has been left open and I can hear Papi and Mickey and Trini whispering. But this polite communication shatters as soon as there's a heavy knock at the door.

"Alfredo," Sheriff Johnson calls out.

"Harold," my father answers. The exchange is somber because this is official business.

"May I have a few words with Maui?" the sheriff says. "Perhaps he can tell us something that will give Isaac's father some hope."

I know what he means: he wants me to tell him Isaac didn't vanish in order to off himself in private.

"He's in his bedroom," Papi says. "This way."

My back is to the door but I can sense the bodies watching me from the entrance.

"Maui," Papi says softly.

"I'm awake," I say.

"Sheriff Johnson would like to talk to you," Papi says. "Tell him everything you know, okay?"

I wrinkle my forehead, annoyed that my father's talking to me like I'm ten years old. But then again, I've been behaving like one.

"I'll wait in the living room," Papi tells Sheriff Johnson.

On any other occasion I'd be thrilled to have the hot sheriff alone in my room. This is like one of my fantasies come true: the big strong lawman comes in to surprise me in bed. But at the moment not even a semi-erection when I feel his weight come down on the bed as he sits down next to me.

"Hey, buddy," Sheriff Johnson. "Rough night, huh?"

Great, another episode of condescension. What is it with these grown-ups?

"Yeah," I answer, because this is what the sheriff wants, for me to chit-chat my way toward some important revelation, though, sadly, I have none.

"The Duttons are mighty upset," Sheriff Johnson says. "They'd like their son back."

I snort with contempt. "I doubt that," I say.

"Oh?" Sheriff Johnson says.

I sit up. I'm pleasantly reminded of why all the women in Caliente fall all over themselves just to get near him. There's plenty to admire: the large brown eyes, the flawless skin, those full lips, strong chin and broad, muscular shoulders. Then there's that scent on him, a mixture of masculine musk and aftershave. It's as if he's doused himself with pheromones. And he's got on his sexy sheriff uniform. Suddenly I do get that semi-erection, so I keep the pillow neatly pressed against my middle.

"What did you mean by that? Was Mr. Dutton hurting Isaac?"

I'm shaken back into reality. "No, not like that," I say. I don't want to get Mr. Dutton in trouble. "Mr. Dutton was hard on Isaac, that's all. He wants Isaac to work at the jewelry store full-time once he finishes high school and that's not what Isaac wants."

"And what does Isaac want?" Sheriff Johnson asks.

"To have his own life. Maybe go away to college or something." I blush as I say this, painfully aware that it's also what I want.

"Maui, uhm," Sheriff Johnson says, becoming uncomfortable. "Does Isaac have a...'friend'?"

Rigoberto González

I look up at him. Oh, brother. "You mean, a boyfriend?"

Sheriff Johnson nods.

"No. He didn't run away to get married, if that's what you're thinking. I don't know where he is or where he could've run off to. This isn't the Isaac I know. He would've told me something. He would've left a note at least or answered his cell phone when I called. I'm his best friend. Or I *thought* I was."

"But you believe Isaac's okay?"

"He's alive, if that's what you mean," I say. "Isaac wouldn't..." I don't dare finish the sentence because I'm not so certain about anything anymore. I sense Sheriff Johnson has learned something also, I can see it in his face. Isaac: queer teenage runaway.

Sheriff Johnson lifts his body off my bed and the mattress rises slightly. "Thank you, Maui," he says. "You've been helpful."

I nod. But before he steps out of my room completely, he turns around and says, "Listen, this is off the subject, and I hope you don't mind my asking."

"Go ahead," I say.

"Do you happen to know if Maddy has a...'friend'?"

Oh, brother. Here we go again. What is it with fathers? Don't they know their own children? Mr. Dutton pushes and pushes and pushes until Isaac falls off the end of the earth and then gets all upset that he can't find his son. My own father walks around like a man with eyes who pretends he can't see. And now this dude comes over completely clueless about his daughter's rebellion—flunking senior year and running around with the ugliest guy in school because her father is the most lusted-after successful man in the valley who has no time for her. Geez!

"I don't know what you mean," I say. This is the part where I act adolescent stupid.

"You know," he says. "A boyfriend! She's been staying out late and last night she showed up—" Sheriff Johnson stops, aware that he has said too much. He smiles. Even his teeth are sexy.

The Mariposa Club

"Well, you take care, Maui," he adds. "I'll let you know if I hear anything important and you do the same. Promise?"

"Promise," I say.

As soon as Sheriff Johnson leaves my room, Trini comes in.

"Hot, huh?" she says.

I roll me eyes. "Now's not the time."

"Oh, you're such a hypocrite," Trini says. "I saw you drooling."

I release a giggle, then tears. Trini comes closer to give me a hug.

"I don't understand," I say. "How could he just leave us like this?"

"Oh, he'll be back tomorrow morning, you watch," Trini says. "Maybe he just drove up to LA to get his ya-yas out at a rave party. It must have been one hell of a fight between him and his father, though. But just wait. Sunday morning he'll show up at church in time to pray for forgiveness."

But that's not what will happen. I can feel it in my soul. I've been feeling it all afternoon. It's a hollow space where my heart used to be.

PART TWO

December Drama

Trini's Beau

The young are said to bounce back so quickly. That may be the case but it sure as shit doesn't mean that it's easy. September came and went, taking with it a heavy load of blues and leaving behind some new ones. I woke up a few times in the middle of the night, thinking that it was Isaac and not Trini who was lying next to me. (Yeah, in case you're wondering, that second guest bed never did make it out of the shed because Aunt Carmen was getting better and soon to be sent home from the hospital. Immediately after, Trini moved back in with her to keep an eye out when a nurse wasn't around. How convenient for Trini's parents.) All I have left of Isaac is a copy of the MISSING flyer the police department made. They could offer nothing more because of Isaac's age—almost eighteen, the low probability that he had been abducted, the high probability that he had run away, which is what we eventually found out thanks to a phone call Isaac made to his mother in the middle of an October night. By then the police had taped a few flyers around the mall so Mr.

Dutton had to take them down himself. I did the same with the flyer that was taped up to the library at school. That's the one I kept and put away. And every time the phone rang for the next few weeks I fantasized that the next phone call Isaac made to the Caliente Valley would be to me. But that didn't happen, which hurt more than his disappearance did.

October came and went, and on Halloween, Trini, Lib, and I had a sleepover and refused to answer the door when the kids in the neighborhood came knocking around to ask for candy. We watched three musicals: Trini selected *Moulin Rouge*, Lib selected *Sweeney Todd*, and I selected *Dancer in the Dark* with Björk in the lead role. They each had varying degrees of downer endings, especially the Björk flick. I guess it was good therapy, given that we were also commemorating our first month without Isaac. So we sat around and cried while we listened to the sad Rufus Wainwright songs and shared funny stories about Isaac as if he had died, which is what this loss was—a kind of death.

Trini laughed. "Remember that time the jocks were harassing us in the locker room and Isaac shut them up by walking up to them completely naked? Even *they* had to respect Isaac's natural talents."

I rolled my eyes, we laughed and then cried. And that's how the night came to a close, with letting everything go. It was like a funeral with flowers and no coffin, a burial with prayers and no grave. And we wished Isaac luck, though the anger of his abandonment never did subside inside of me.

The Fierce Foursome is now a trio but it's a three-legged stumble all the way. For one thing, without Isaac we've been forced to ride the bus—the ultimate senior year indignity. We were back to being the fags that ride in the front because all the tough kids claim the back. Every once in a while the occasional spit wad, but usually just the knowing glances as soon as Trini and I stepped inside. But that was only for the first few weeks. Now that Trini's back at Aunt Carmen's she rides Paulina Rubio, the old station wagon, to school. I catch a ride whenever I can.

The novelty has worn off about Lib as well, though it took some time for everyone on his bus route (and in the school for that matter) to get used to his Goth eyeliner and black fingernails. Plus, he's somewhat of a celebrity because of his smarts. Any little accomplishment of his makes the school paper.

And at the risk of sounding cliché, I must be honest and say that not everything is doom and gloom. For one thing, I took over for Isaac at Joyería Dutton. My Spanish comes in handy and it seems to be a way for Mr. Dutton to believe that not everything is lost. I get paid at the end of each week and I set that money aside because my dream now is to buy a used car by the time I graduate. Perhaps if I contribute toward a down payment Papi will be more likely to help out.

Most surprising of all, Mr. Dutton doesn't even bat an eye to Trini hanging around the jewelry store once in a while. She cleans up the display cases the way I used to when Isaac was in charge. Mr. Dutton even tried to make conversation with her once but it was so awkward for both of them that now they usually keep their exchanges simple—hello and goodbye. I guess it takes a crisis to put things in perspective. What did Mr. Dutton gain by being cold and insensitive to his gay son and his gay friends? Only heartache.

Accepting Mr. Dutton's afterschool job offer is also my way of believing that I'm only holding Isaac's place until he returns. Poor Mr. Dutton. Sometimes when business is slow his mind drifts and he looks off into space. Who knows what conversations he's having in his head? Who knows how much he would give to make it all right again?

Since I'm now starting my second month on the job, Mr. Dutton has gotten more comfortable doing his thing in the back room while I mind the store on my own. I'm really just there to show people the inexpensive pieces and to call him in if a transaction's going to happen. No biggie. And since Christmas shopping season is still weeks away, the mall is relatively quiet, except for Trini, who's always within earshot no matter where she's standing.

Celie passes the store. "Let's go, guys, step it up," she says, as she follows Los Calis out of the mall.

"Looking good, Celie!" Trini yells out, waving.

"Look at that fag!" one of the gang members says.

Trini blows them a kiss and waves. She makes her way over, wearing Mickey's hand-me-down sunglasses and with a diaphanous blue scarf wrapped around her neck. "What do you think? Too Audrey Hepburn? Not enough María Félix?"

"Who?" I say.

"Really, Maui," she says, taking off the sunglasses. "If you're going to be a fag of the twenty-first century, your frame of reference needs to expand to include all knowledge of fag culture from the ancient twentieth century. Otherwise you're without history, context or queer lineage. Furthermore, you have twice the responsibility because you're a brown fag—a *reina*—so your sissy savvy needs to encompass the entirety of the Americas. That's in English, Spanish, and everything between the butt cheeks. Snap!"

"All righty, then," I say. "So, is the bicultural Diva too fierce to wipe some fingerprints off the glass?"

"Rub-a-dub-dub, can I see *him* in the tub?" Trini says under her breath.

A guy in his mid-twenties walks in wearing a plaid shirt opened to expose the dark hair on his flat chest. His jeans are comfortably tight, bringing out all the right curves and, uhm, bulges. The hairline is receding, but we don't hold that against him.

"Good afternoon, sir," Trini says. "How can we help you? Looking for anything special?"

Rigoberto González

The guy smiles knowingly at Trini. "Kind of, sort of," he says. "I lost one of my studs, so I'd like to replace it." He points to his earlobes. Both are pierced but one of them is missing an earring.

"That's a stud all right," Trini says. I groan. And before I have a chance to point out the location of the stud earrings, Trini takes over.

"This way, please," Trini says. "Take your time now. We wouldn't want you going away too quickly." The guy laughs.

That's when I realize this is not the typical run-of-the-mill straight dude, otherwise he would've already fled. Trini's coming on too strong and the guy is eating it up. I'm actually impressed, and a little jealous. So this is how it works? Though I can't imagine myself as flirty as Trini, who's now fluttering around her new conquest like an intoxicated butterfly.

As if on cue, the third member of our group swoops in from around the corner.

"Oh. My. Goddess," Lib says. "Who's *that*? I saw him coming in and I just had to see it for myself."

"Geez. You've got gaydar *and* sonar? I didn't even know you were in the mall," I say.

"How old do you think he is? Twenty-five?"

"Abouts," I say. "It's hard to tell with the hairline. I don't remember seeing him around."

When Lib puts his head close to mine I finally notice it: he has a pierced lip.

"When did *that* happen?" I say, pointing at it.

"Last night," Lib said. "One of Celie's friends has this portable tattoo kit and piercing equipment, so I made the leap into true Goth punk."

"And your parents were okay with it?"

Lib does his cocky head-swiveling. "Not really," he says. "But what can they do? I'm like graduating from high school one year early, I've already got college recruiters tracking me down, *and*

Principal Boozely called me up himself to inform me that *I* am the new class valedictorian!"

"Biiitch," I say, extending the word in respect. "Sounds like everything's falling into place. I'm very happy for you." Though I mean it, I can't help feeling a tinge of envy.

"Thank you, Maui, that means a lot to me coming from you."

I reach up to feel the hoop. Lib draws his head back. "Don't touch it! It's still tender."

"Did it hurt?" I ask.

"Of course it did," Lib says. "I had to sleep on my back, which was hard."

When Trini finally makes her way over after the guy leaves, she's glowing.

"Guess what, girls?" she says. "I gave him my number!"

"Hey, Juliet," I say. "This is a place of business! Did you try to make a sale at least?"

"Oh, he'll be back tomorrow or something, he's just—" Trini stops at mid-sentence.

"What?" Lib says, caught by her stare.

"What's that piece of wire doing sticking out of your face?" Trini says.

"I got my lip pierced," Lib says. "It's an expression of my individuality and independence."

Trini rolls her eyes. "Well, you better hold on to that. It's the only penetration you'll be getting for a while."

"Hey!" I say, doing my loud whisper thing. "Mr. Dutton's in the back room."

"Well, I'm taking off," Lib says. "I've got something brewing that I'm sure you will appreciate. Details tomorrow at school."

"Bye-bye, metal face," Trini says, waving.

Lib flashes the middle finger as he leaves the jewelry store.

"I wish you would be nicer to him," I say. "He's becoming quite a superstar, you know."

Rigoberto González

Trini shrugs her shoulders, pretending she's not jealous. I purse my lips. I guess we all have our flaws.

"Anyway, back to more pressing matters," Trini says, getting all giddy again. "Do you think he'll really call?"

"Trini, he's like ten years older than you. And, actually, now that we're on the subject, technically, you're not even of legal age to—you know."

"To what?"

"Buy cigarettes," I say, deadpan. "You know what I mean!"

"Oh, Passion Flower. One day I will explain to you why some of us sit with our legs open, and others, like you, still have to sit with your legs crossed."

"Well, I don't know, Trini," I say. "Just be careful."

"I'll come by later, maybe. I need to take Aunt Carmen to get some blood work at the clinic. Ciao!"

I sigh. Isaac is still the only one I've ever had any kind of physical contact with, and though I've had plenty of masturbatory fantasies about anonymous encounters and surprise visits by members of the local law enforcement in the middle of night, I'm not really ready for anything beyond that. A few passersby catch my eye, mainly the Latino boys with shaved heads and the surfer blondes with white stone necklaces and skateboards, and—to quote Trini—"everything between the butt cheeks." But that's all: catalogue browsing without commitment.

The back room door opens and Mr. Dutton steps out looking like he has aged twenty years in the last two months.

"Maui," he says. "We're going to close the shop early today."

I look at my watch. We still have a little over an hour before closing time. "Are you okay, Mr. Dutton?"

He waves away my question and nods his head. I'm not sure how to interpret those gestures, but I assume he doesn't want to talk about it. He takes out his keys and starts moving the valuable items to the safe in the back. I step out from behind the display cases to slide the security barriers down.

"Would you like a ride to your house?" Mr. Dutton says, but I have a feeling his offer is only a courtesy, that he really just wants to get home.

"I'm fine," I say. "I've got a friend coming back to pick me up. I'll wait at the food court and do my homework." I grab my back pack.

Mr. Dutton nods. I lock the barriers from the outside, the lights inside the store and display cases go off, and I'm stuck in the Lame View Mall for the next hour or so, waiting for Trini to return. I suppose I could walk home but it's still a little too warm to do that. Screw it. I decide to have a cheap mall dinner and then take the city bus home.

After I order my teriyaki chicken on fried rice with a large drink, I sit at one of the generic food court tables. The thing about senior year in high school is that there's not as much homework. I guess the teachers figure if they haven't taught us by now we'll never learn. I've already taken the SAT but only because we're all required to, those of us who are "college-bound," that is. Lib's all excited about getting his scores; Trini, who chose not to take the test, scoffs each time the subject comes up.

Minutes later, I'm absent-mindedly scooping up rice and reading up on the next chapter of chemistry, when I suddenly have this strange feeling that I'm being watched. I look around. It's Trini's beau sitting a few tables across from me. When he smiles and waves I nearly choke on my plastic fork.

"Hey, I didn't mean to startle you," he says as soon as he comes up to my table. "May I sit?"

"For a few minutes," I say. "I need to finish my homework."

"Understood, understood," he says. "I was just curious about why the jewelry store closed early today. I came back to make my purchase."

Rigoberto González

"Oh," I say, my mind at ease after the explanation. "I have no idea, actually. Mr. Dutton's been in a strange mood lately so I just follow his orders."

"You like following orders?" he says. His sheepish grin makes me uncomfortable. That little alarm that goes off in the back of the brain, the one that has been silent for years but which came in handy back in the days of my childhood when my parents said things like "Don't talk to strangers"—*that* alarm? It starts to ring.

"I'm David, by the way," he says, extending his hand. David is charming. I can see why Trini melted so quickly. But there's something odd lurking behind his eyes.

The fact that we're in a public space allows me to overcome my hesitation and shake hands with him. "I'm Maui," I say. "I'm a good friend of Trini's."

"Who?" he says, and I know he's lying, playing with me.

"Trini," I say. "You met her—him at the jewelry store. He gave you his number."

"Oh, yes, Trini, yes," David says. "He must have misunderstood me. But I was asking for the number of the store. I didn't want to burst his bubble, though. You know what I mean." He winks at me and I blush.

"Would it be too much to ask if you could give me *your* number?" David says.

My body freezes. This is not a flattering exchange at all. I wish Isaac were here, or even Lib. This guy wouldn't even have dared come near if I was not alone.

"You mean the number of the jewelry store? Sure," I say. Two can play this game.

David laughs. "I catch your drift," he says, and then he brings his head closer and breathes in deeply. "And it smells naughty."

"I need to go," I say. I stand up, but before I have time to move, David grabs my arm and locks it in place against the table top. I'm stunned by his aggressiveness.

"So soon?" he asks. "But we're having such a wonderful conversation. Please, have a seat."

Like a fool I sit back down. "What do you want from me?"

"I just want to talk to you, get acquainted, that's all," David says. "Is that so bad? No, of course not."

I'm feeling trapped. "Take your hand off my arm, please," I say. David complies.

"So what do you do for fun?" David asks.

The doublespeak is getting annoying. Somehow I can't imagine that this is how he talked with Trini.

"I go to school, I go to work, I go home," I say. "There isn't really time for fun. I'm only seventeen. I'm still a minor."

"Oh, that shouldn't stop you," David says. "I started screwing when I was fourteen."

My body tenses up. The word "screwing" coming out of his mouth sounds vulgar and threatening.

"What's the matter?" David says, his tone seductive. "Did that scare you? You've never heard anyone talk like that before? *Screwing! Screw-ing!*"

I understand now why he's picked me—somehow that bigmouth Trini let it slip that I'm a virgin. But it's not Trini's fault that this SOB is messing with my head.

"You like to screw?" I say, charged with anger. "Go screw yourself!"

I quickly grab my things and take off, leaving my unfinished dinner behind with David, who's more amused than insulted. Rushing off I don't dare look back. I want to be at home. I want to be at school. I want to be in a safe place where men like this are not allowed to enter. Suddenly, I see my savior, Celie.

Rigoberto González

"Celie! Celie!" I call out, and she turns to me and smiles through her white Goth face. I'm safe again. I feel safe. Safe. For the moment.

When I walk out to the bus stop, I pause just short of the shelter because there's a guy inside wearing the tell-tale baggy pants and oversized jacket of our Caliente Valley gang members. Tony Sánchez sits at the bench, smoking a cigarette. He's the youngest dope-dealing member of Los Calis, and I know for a fact he's not waiting for the bus. I decide to stand close, but not too close.

"Wassup?" Tony says to me.

"Not much," I say. To calm my nerves a bit, I'm about to volunteer more information, but then my common sense kicks in and I keep my mouth shut.

"Smoke?" he says, holding up his cigarette box.

I shake my head, confused all of a sudden by the attention. Suddenly I can appreciate the value of technology at times like this: a cell phone or an iPod would keep me distracted and excused from any sort of interaction. But like many high school kids in Caliente, these luxuries are not ours to have—not at our age.

So I resort to pulling a book out of my backpack. Not the most effective alternative but it's the more inconspicuous gesture available to me. I open up a copy of Sophocles' play *Oedipus Rex*.

"You're a schoolboy, aren't you?" Tony says to me.

I hear "nerd," I hear "geek" when he says "schoolboy," but it's not like I can argue. Or want to.

"I didn't mean it like that," Tony says, as if he has read my thoughts through the expression on my face. "I just meant you like school."

"It's all right," I say. I'm not supposed to say that I do.

"You want to sit?" he asks, moving over on the bench.

"I'm okay," I say.

"No, come on," he insists. "Sit. I've seen you standing at the jewelry store all afternoon."

If this is a test then I know I'm going to fail. If it's a trap or a mind game, I know I'm already caught in whatever web has been spun. Like an idiot who doesn't know better, I sit. My heartbeat quickens.

Tony laughs. "Relax, homeboy," he says to me. For a second I think he has just said "homo," but thankfully I don't react.

I keep my face locked to the street, and once in a while I turn to the left, hoping that I'll see my bus coming down the avenue.

After about five minutes of silence, I have the courage to turn my head slightly to the right. I have never been this close to one of Los Calis before. Away from the group, Tony doesn't seem that threatening, but I'm still apprehensive, mostly because of all the rumors that he, like all the other gang members, carries a concealed weapon. I don't know if he does or if he doesn't, but I have to play it safe either way.

"You have a girl, buddy?" Tony asks, and I'm thrown back to the paralyzing suspicion that he's toying with me.

Of course, I don't have a girl! Everyone, including Tony, has seen me sitting on the Queer Planter all this time along with Isaac, Trini, and Lib, who also don't have—and will never have—girls because we *are* the girls.

Finally I shake my head.

"That's all right," Tony says.

He pulls out his wallet, opens it up and shows me a photograph of a girl with thinly-plucked eyebrows and teased hair. "She's mine. Pretty, isn't she?" Tony says. And I'm forced to nod.

When Tony looks at me, I recognize the longing. My anxiety dissipates and turns to pity. Tony's trying very hard to pass himself off as a tough guy among Los Calis, and as a straight boy in front of me. It must be hard to pretend to be who he wants people to believe he is.

Rigoberto González

"Her name's Amanda," Tony says.

He loses himself in thoughts of Amanda and I seize the chance to look at him closely. Tony's not bad-looking at all, but he has hidden himself inside this disguise—a buzz cut and a pencil-thin mustache that hasn't quite reached the thick hair stage. His lips are full, delicate, and kissable.

Suddenly he turns around and locks eyes with me. His face softens, as if this stare-down has seduced the tenderness out of it. And all of a sudden everything around us melts away. No Caliente, no Lame View Mall, no bus shelter, not even the clothing over our bodies stand between the possibility of our skins touching.

Tony breaks into a smile. Not a malicious one or a knowing one, but a genuine smile. "You don't remember, do you?" he says.

My head snaps back in surprise. "Remember what?" I say.

Tony chuckles. "You really don't remember."

And then it all comes back to me: we *have* kissed. Elementary school, third grade, recess. It was more of an accident than anything else. Or rather it began that way. A group of us was playing hide-and-seek and Tony and I squeezed our bodies inside the stack of tires painted blue. We squatted there in silence, facing each other, knees touching and refusing to even twitch. A minute later, anxious about how well-hidden we were, Tony wanted to peek, so he started to lift his body up and I pulled him down by his shirt. When he plopped back down, his chin struck my mouth. He realized I had been hurt and pressed his hand over my lips. And just as tenderly, he leaned forward and comforted me by kissing my wound.

"I remember," I say, finally, blushing.

"Those were the innocent days," Tony says, and he sighs the sigh of an old man reaching back decades. "Don't you wish it was all that simple again?"

"Yeah," I say, matching his wistful reflection. I have the urge then to make some kind of body contact, like resting my hand

The Mariposa Club

on his shoulder or something, since we have torn down, at least temporarily, the barriers that adolescence has forced us to raise. It wouldn't be a sexual gesture at all, just one of empathy: *I know what you're talking about, man. I feel you.* But just as I'm about to move my arm toward that gesture, the bus comes screeching to a stop in front of us, breaking apart the euphoric spell.

I jump and reach into my pocket for bus fare.

"Take it easy, man," Tony says to me, his voice heavy with tough-guy attitude. He has put the mask back on.

I don't answer. I quickly climb on the bus, deposit my cash, and then drop my body on the seat. I don't exhale again until the bus driver closes the doors and shifts into gear. It is only when the bus starts to move that I dare look toward the shelter, which looks like a glass closet or a glass coffin. And Tony sits inside, motionless and expressionless, as the shelter gets farther away and smaller until it finally shrinks out of view.

Rigoberto González

Mariposa Mission

The next morning Lib greets me as soon as I get off the bus. He's got a portfolio under one arm and a small Day of the Dead lunch box he uses as an all-purpose storage space. Everything from cookies to erasers gets tossed around inside. A bit melodramatic, if you ask me, but it's all part of this image he's cultivating as the eccentric school brain. He waves at me, as if he's difficult to spot.

"Maui," he says. "I wanted to talk to you face to face about an important matter. Come, let's take a seat in my office."

How the Queer Planter became Lib's office is beyond me, though the space has been up for grabs since we stopped hanging around it ever since Isaac left. Since Lib and Trini get along even less now, we only regroup on occasion.

"So, I've been thinking," Lib says, lowering his head as if he's plotting something big. "We need to revisit the Mariposa Club."

The Mariposa Club. Up until now I haven't even thought about it.

"I don't know, Lib," I say. "It didn't go over so well the last time. And besides, our potential membership has dwindled some."

Lib shakes his head. "You need to keep it positive, girl. The reason it didn't work the last time is that we got all distracted."

He takes out the club application form and hands it to me. At the top he's written: *The Mariposa Club: A Gay/Straight Alliance.*

"Wait," I say. "What happened to the LGBT part?"

"Get with the times, Maui. Let's face it, an LGBT club in *this* school, in *this* town, was only going to corral the Fierce Foursome a few photo-ops. But an *alliance—that's* revolutionary!"

"Revolutionary?" I say. "All righty, then. Bust out the cannons."

"I've been doing some research and, not surprisingly, we're behind the times here in the Caliente Valley. All over the country it's all about making these issues *everyone's* issues. I mean, for crying out loud, we're still fighting for gay marriage, and for the right for gay couples to adopt children or be foster parents." As his excitement grows, Lib starts to get louder and louder. "An alliance at the high school level is that important first step towards educating the future voters of America about *every* queer person's rights!"

Lib raises his arms in triumph.

I arch my eyebrows. "Where's all this coming from?"

"What do you mean?" he asks.

"All of a sudden you're like the Barack Obama of Caliente Valley High or something. Have you been sniffing your nail polish again?"

Lib chuckles. "Maui, let me explain something," he says, pulling out a copy of *Out* magazine for an impromptu show and tell. "It says here we members of Generation Q have a bright future ahead of us if we go out and take it. Just a few months ago I was content jerking off to Mario López on YouTube. But today, I feel the urge to do something meaningful and productive post-You-

Rigoberto González

Tube orgasm. It's about time we grew up and joined the big fights out there because, face it: the real world is only months away for us. You want to go out there like a doofus, or like a diva?"

"Okay, I need to see what you've been reading, kid," I say, reaching for the magazine. "You sound like you just got brain-washed."

"Maui, please," Lib says, pulling the magazine away. "Think about it. I'm taking this to a public forum and I would really like your support."

I sit still for a moment, perplexed and slightly impressed by Lib's new sense of purpose, though I'm not quite sure what he means about "a public forum."

"We'll revisit it during study hour," I say. "Hey, listen, I had the weirdest encounter with that guy from the jewelry store last night."

"Trini's new boyfriend?"

"Well, yes and no," I say, and then I proceed to tell my sordid tale of the creepy seduction at the food court.

"You see?" Lib says. "*This* is why we need to have a space to have these difficult conversations: so that our underage queers know what to do to avoid becoming victims of these kamika-ze predators! And what about Isaac? Have you forgotten about Isaac? Also a victim of ignorance and homophobia—in his own home, even!"

"I wasn't victimized!" I say. "You know, you're spinning this way out of control."

Thankfully, Trini comes strolling by, wearing a different pair of sunglasses that match her red long-sleeved blouse. She keeps one arm pressed against her tote bag. "Morning, girls," she says. She removes the sunglasses and poses. "Notice anything different?"

"You bathed?" Lib says.

Trini winces at him. "Shouldn't you be updating your profile on Chubby Chasers 'R' Us? You look a little heavier."

The Mariposa Club

"Broomsticks and headstones, Trini," Lib says. "Names will never hurt me."

"Trini," I say, "I was just telling Lib about David, the guy from the jewelry store yesterday—"

"Oh, *David*," Trini says. "Did he come back to buy his stud? He said he would. I spent all evening on this facial. As you can clearly see. If you want to keep a man, you've got to give him something to come back to. Not that either of you would know."

"Trini," I say. "I think you need—"

"Yes," Lib interrupts. "I do notice something different. A kind of glow about you, a radiance, even. You look great!"

Both Trini and I look puzzled by Lib's sudden change in tone.

"Well, thank you," Trini says, surprised by the compliment. "It's a new product, imported from Mexico."

"You mean the pharmacy across the border where Aunt Carmen gets her discount meds?" I say.

"If it crosses the international line, it's an import, dummy," Trini says. "Anyway, it's a new line too cutting edge for the U.S., so it can only be smuggled into the country. I've only used it a few times and the results are, shall we say, *magnifique*."

"So," Lib says, elbowing me. "Did David call you last night? How exciting! Tell us all about it."

"Lib—"

"Shh! Let her speak," Lib says. "Well?"

"Well, not exactly," Trini says. "I mean, he's busy. But I know he'll be getting in touch this afternoon. So, Maui, I'm afraid I won't be coming to the mall with you. I can drop you off but that's it. I wouldn't want to miss David's phone call."

"No, you shouldn't," Lib says. "If it's one thing I've learned from you is not to let an opportunity pass me by."

"Right," Trini says, wrinkling her brow in confusion. "Well, if you want your own bottle of beauty cream, let me know. I'll be

Rigoberto González

taking orders before Aunt Carmen's next trip to the border. See you at study hour."

As soon as Trini is out of earshot I slap Lib on the shoulder.

"That was cruel," I say. "I think she should know about David."

"What for?" Lib says. "Let her have her moment. She'll move on soon enough."

The bell rings and Lib picks up his portfolio. "Remember to think about what I just told you!" he says. "It'll be a whole new Mariposa Mission!"

I shake my head. These two are something else.

First period chemistry is a blur because we have a substitute teacher yet again—some science geeko who still wears suspenders. Our beloved Ms. Disaster has been out periodically because of some back problem, and rumor has it that Boozely wants to retire her by the semester break because she's so old.

Honors English with Mr. Doze is yet another sleeping pill dropped into the hour of fine literature. He drones on and on about Greek mythology, which he manages to make boring despite the high drama, murders, monsters, bestial seductions, and homosexual encounters. Lib has been paying more attention in class and raises his hand often, bringing unwanted attention to our outsider table. Snake and Maddy glare at him. They have had to put aside their text messaging, but by now everyone knows they're a couple so they simply sit there, counting down the minutes like I do, in anticipation of study hour. And when it finally arrives it's like the classroom is a closet that has just spit out its cluster of trapped moths.

"Fresh air!" I say.

"Fascinating stuff," Lib declares. "You know, Greek mythology and the Bible are probably the backbone of Western literature.

They're referenced and alluded to by every major writer in Western history!"

"Lib, cut it out, already," I say. "It's getting annoying."

"What's annoying? My vested interest in my education?"

"No, your non-stop ra-ra-ra 'look at me I'm so special' attitude," I say. "I mean, we know you're the class genius, okay? No need to flash your I.Q. at us every time we look at you."

Lib stops and gives me the shiny eyeball.

"What?" I say. "You know, for someone who walks around in vampire drag, you sure have thin skin."

"Maui," Lib says. "You know what your problem is? You just shoot your mouth off without accepting responsibility for what you say. How many times have we been through this little scenario? You kick and scream, say mean things to us, and then come back whimpering that you didn't mean it. Seriously, you've got anger-management issues. I still love you, though. I accept you as you are and I hope you realize your shortcomings and become a better person. That will help *you* love yourself."

Lib walks ahead of me and leaves me feeling disoriented despite the fact that I think he's been watching a little too much *Oprah* recently and taking too many good notes. Something inside me tells me I should catch up and apologize, but I don't. I suppose it's one of those "shortcomings" he just mentioned. I know right from wrong and I *still* choose to ignore it. Hmm, that sounded Oprah-ish too. I guess clarity's contagious.

When I get to the library, Grump is on the prowl trying to find someone to snap at for chewing gum or loitering between the stacks or for coughing too loudly. He's a strange old man with a quick temper, and probably the most-despised adult in the school. Lib is sitting down in a cubicle, which is his way of telling me that he needs his space right now, and I don't blame him. I take a seat at one of the open tables and wait for Trini. A few tables over, Snake and Maddy play footsie.

Rigoberto González

Grump clears his throat. He reaches down for his coffee mug and takes a drink. Suddenly the sliding doors open and in comes Hotter in all his glory.

"Good morning, Mr. Trotter," Grump says in a soft voice that doesn't quite match his usual disposition.

"Mr. Gump, good morning," Mr. Trotter says. "I was wondering if I could put this book on reserve." When he holds out the book, his biceps and pecs bulge right through his fitted dress shirt. To quote Trini, *Rub-a-dub-dub*.

"Oh, yes, certainly," Grump says, the glee in his voice is unmistakable.

I blink a few times: Am I really witnessing this? Is it really respect that Grump is offering Hotter? Or something else? Old man Grump keeps his eyes on Hotter as Hotter nods his head in gratitude and then turns around to exit, giving both Grump and me an awesome view of his tight, muscular ass. All the while, Hotter seems to be clueless that not only is the old cantankerous librarian checking him out, but so is the skinny Mexican kid from his fifth period class.

And then the spell is broken when Grump notices that *I'm* noticing his temporary drift into man-butt-cheek ecstasy. He looks back at me, his face collapsed into its familiar curmudgeon mask.

"Let's get to work," he says. I nod and crack open the closest book within reach.

The sliding doors open again, and I know Grump is as hopeful as I am that Mr. Trotter has returned: maybe he gave the wrong book, maybe he forgot his favorite pen, maybe he just wants to give us another look. But, no, this time it's Trini.

"You're ten minutes late to study hour, young man," Grump says.

"So sorry," Trini says. "I'm new here and I just now found the library. You know, the school should really provide maps." She then looks around the room as if it's her first time. "Nice digs!" she says.

Grump is unconvinced but decides to let it go.

"Where's Lib?" Trini says. "Memorizing the Gettysburg Address?"

As Trini settles in, sifting through her tote bag for this and that, I take a sideways glance at Grump—Mr. Gump, that is. Poor sad Mr. Gump. He sits down and picks up a book to read, all the while keeping his ears peeled for the slightest disruption that will give him reason to bark. But there's a sadness there too. Who knows what his story is? All I know is that one of his simple pleasures must be watching Hotter walk in and out of his domain. All I know is that that's one of my simple pleasures as well.

God, is that what I'll become? An angry bitter old queen eyeing the math teacher? As opposed to being what? An angry bitter young queen eyeing the math teacher? What does Mr. Gump have to be angry about? What's *my* beef?

I resolve right then and there that I will—yet again—apologize to Lib. And that I'll help him on this new Mariposa Mission of his, whatever it is as long as it doesn't cut into my social life. Ha ha.

I'm about to turn around to get Lib's attention when I suddenly hear the sniffling. Not the kind of sniffling that comes from an allergy or a cold, but from a kick to the heart. Two tables down, Maddy's face is quickly getting wet. Snake sits next to her looking like he doesn't have the slightest idea how to comfort her.

"There's something never seen before," Trini whispers.

I'm at a loss myself. But I'm more annoyed that Snake doesn't make a move either. Matters worsen when Maddy breaks out into a full-blown bawl.

Even Grump looks stunned. "Young lady," he says. "Is there a problem?"

"I'll say," Trini says.

Rigoberto González

"Maddy!" Snake says. "Keep it down."

"Up yours, Walter!" Maddy screams and runs out of the library.

"Miss, miss," Grump calls out. "Study hour's not over yet."

"Please," Trini says with a dismissive wave of her hand. "Nothing's going to stop that runaway train."

Snake slumps down into his arms and bangs one fist against the table. By this time Grump has figured out that something bigger than the library rules is going on and simply keeps quiet, observing from a distance.

Lib can't resist and breaks out of his cubicle to sit with Trini and me. "High drama," he says.

"Walter?" Trini says. "Who knew?"

"I wonder what that's about," I say.

"Hello?" Trini says. "It's like, a break-up? Poor thing. Even lesbians have feelings you know."

Lib scoffs. "She's *not* a lesbian. Not with this guy, anyway."

"We'll I'm surprised she didn't crack his head open on the spot," I say.

"Tragic," Trini says. "It makes me appreciate my Davy Wavy more than ever."

Lib and I look at each other. I have the urge to smile, but not because I want to make fun of Trini's delusional relationship, but because Lib and I are speaking again.

"Hey," Lib says. "We need to do another DVD night."

I nod. "Sure. What will be our theme?"

"Star-crossed lovers?" Trini offers.

"Repressed homosexuality," I say.

"Delusional romance," Lib says.

"Boys!" Gump yells out. And that makes us burst out laughing.

Once we quiet down, we settle back into our seats to pretend we're studying, but this is the time of the day we simply reflect. I imagine Trini has his mind full of Davy Wavy and Aunt Carmen; Lib is spinning his political wheels; and I'm simply sitting here trying to make sense of the complicated creature we call the gay man: Isaac, David, Mr. Gump, and Tony Sánchez—Tony Sánchez who has been sitting in the corner of the library all along, watching me.

I gulp down my dry Adam's apple. Tony looks kind of cute from this safe distance. He makes me want to blow him a kiss. But then when Tony lifts his hand to wave, a cold chill runs down my spine. I don't want to wave back, so I simply nod to acknowledge him without letting Trini or Lib notice our exchange. I lower my head to force my eyes onto the strict, non-wandering paths of print.

Yes, such complicated creatures we all are.

Rigoberto González

Mayor Liberace García

By the end of the week, I have my doubts again about this whole Mariposa Mission thing. Where do I start?

Mr. Mad Publicity himself started posting up flyers everywhere about the need for a gay/straight alliance organization in Caliente Valley High. But to maximize the impact, he decorated the notices with red ribbons, pink triangles, and rainbow flags. Needless to say, these were seldom seen symbols around these parts, and as soon as they went up they began to be torn down or defaced, which was slightly more tolerable than coming across them with anti-gay graffiti like "*Die fagots!*" Pointing out the misspelling, Trini said, "You *know* the remedial morons wrote that one."

Then Lib has the bright idea of putting together a sandwich board with the same message and wearing it around during lunch hour. This elicits more than a few anonymous slurs flung from the crowd and more than a share of snickers. Boozely comes around to ask him to stop parading around with it because it's a distraction. And Lib, ever the rule-follower, complies, but with the request that he wants to hold an informational booth during the club fair. Boozely has no choice, but it's clear he's not happy about it.

"What's he so afraid of?" Trini asks.

"He's afraid Lib is going to get us killed," I say.

We help Lib make the sign for the table, which gets tucked neatly at the end of the row and partially hidden by a hedge, and then we sit there, the three of us, getting no love from the high school community.

"This is ridiculous," Lib says. "No one can even see us back here. I mean, they gave the military recruiters the prime spots near the quad."

"You do have to admit," Trini says. "They *are* kind of cute."

Lib steps out from behind the table and stands at the center of the walkway to distribute the pamphlets no one has stepped forward to pick up.

"The Mariposa Club: A Gay/Straight Alliance, people!" Lib calls out. "The Mariposa Club: A Gay/Straight Alliance. It's about time we take some responsibility."

The few students who walk by ignore him or refuse to accept the pamphlets.

"You're wasting your time," Trini says. "No one here gives a shit."

"Gay/Straight Alliance!"

"He's persistent, I'll say that," I offer.

Student after student walks by, none giving much thought to Lib's invitations to accept the pamphlet. And then Tony Sánchez walks by. Lib hands him a pamphlet.

Tony takes a glance at it. "What the hell is this?"

"It's an informational pamphlet on establishing a gay/straight alliance in our school."

"Oh, shit," I say.

Rigoberto González

Tony rips the pamphlet in half and throws the pieces at Lib. "Damn homos!" he says as he stomps away.

"You would know," Lib says under his breath.

Tony stomps back. "What did you just say?"

Trini, never one to back out of a conflict, steps in. "Oh, come off it, girl," she says to Tony. I squirm in my seat.

"Say what?"

"You *know* there's a flaming mariposa tucked away in there just screaming to break out of the cocoon and live among the rainbows," Trini says. She does her hand-crossing, thumb-locking, finger-fluttering thing.

I break out into an instant sweat. "Trini, *no.*"

And before anyone else has a chance to say anything else, Tony kicks our table, which collapses on my feet.

"Shit!" I yell out in pain.

"Lib, this punk just squashed Maui!" Trini yells out.

"You need to back up, you," Lib says to Tony and Tony retaliates by pushing Lib, whose body twists over as he falls on top of the table and on top of me.

"Aah!" I yell out.

"Hate crime in progress! Hate crime in progress!" Trini yells out, swinging her tote bag at Tony.

In a flash, campus security arrives on the scene and so does everybody else who had previously ignored us. The crowd closes in around us.

"Back it up! Back it up!" the security guard yells out, holding our assailant by the arm.

"I didn't kill nobody!" Tony says. "Damn queers deserved it!"

"Watch your mouth, buddy," the security guard says.

Tony surrenders to the security guard, who walks him off to the administration office.

Boozely points an accusing finger. "I'll be right with you, Mr. Sánchez!"

The Mariposa Club

"I want to file a grievance," Lib says to the principal. The new piercing on his lip cut into his gums when he fell and is now bleeding profusely from his mouth. "Do you see, citizens of CV High?" he says, turning to the other kids. "Do you see now what we're up against?"

"Lib, you're spitting blood all over the place when you talk!" Trini says.

"What in the world?" says Boozely, reacting to the blood-gushing. "Mr. García, what's this?"

"Well, Principal Beasley," Lib says, holding his hand over his mouth. "That young man just demonstrated to our community the lack of tolerance that continues to thrive in our school. This is not the high school *I* want to attend."

"He's right!" a voice in the crowd calls out.

"Yeah, what the hell? He didn't have to beat him up just because he's a queer," says another sympathetic voice.

"Thanks," I say with sarcasm in my voice. I'm up on my feet, no harm done, except that Lib's weight sprained my ankle. Lib, however, keeps bleeding. "Lib, you need to get that looked at right away," I say.

"Let's get you to the nurse," the second security guard chimes in, guiding him away by the arm.

Boozely shakes his head in disgust. "You see? You see? This is just the kind of trouble I wanted to avoid."

"Hey, wait a minute," Trini says. "You can't blame the victim and not the bully. This is *so* not fair."

"Yeah," says a voice from the crowd. "It's not their fault."

As Trini helps me limp over to sit down on one of the planters, I sense a different tide moving through the student body. Not that they'll all start taking pamphlets or something, but this is exactly the kind of momentum that's going to fuel Lib's gay/straight alliance effort. This is a small school with a graduating class of a couple of hundred people. Incidents of violence are rare here, so

Rigoberto González

this one's going to make an impact. I can feel it. But part of me feels sorry for Tony, who probably got scared coming too close to our group of flamers. I mean, he's one of us, but not in the same way.

"All right, all right," Boozely says. "Nothing left to see, let's all finish lunch hour and get to class on time."

The crowd disperses and Boozely heads back to the administration office, shaking his head again. A few of our fellow classmates help put our table back together and collect our scattered pamphlets.

"Thank you," I say, slightly embarrassed by the sudden attention. "Thank you."

"Poor Lib," Trini says. "She got herself cut the hell up."

I wince. I decide to leave it alone because even if Trini *did* say something stupid to Tony there was no need for Tony to get physical.

"Are you okay to walk, dude," a jock says as he comes up. "That was frickin' awesome, man. We never get to see any action around here."

Although I'm slightly flattered that I just earned some street cred, I'm still in pain. "I think I need some ice," I say.

"Here, lean on me," the jock says. "I'll take you."

I put my weight on his shoulder as Trini looks on with a combination of surprise and envy.

"Don't drop him," she warns.

I can't help turning my head and flashing her my mischievous smile.

At the nurse's office, Lib lies down on the examination table, pressing a bloody wet rag over his mouth, gauze shoved inside his swollen lip. Nurse Helga Milkovich—that's Nurse Helga to her face—hands me a bag of ice.

"You boys," she says through a gravelly voice. "You play so rough out there! You should be more careful. Now you're going home to break your mothers' hearts. How did this happen? Football?"

Lib lets out a muffled chuckle. But Nurse Helga, the old clueless lady with the Band-Aids, doesn't expect an answer. She simply comes in and out of her office, mostly to talk to herself.

"Well, this is lovely," I say. "Though on the bright side, I think that's the closest we've ever come to straight boy action."

Lib pulls the rags out of his mouth each time he wants to talk. "Did you see what happened out there? I think we got ourselves an audience."

"Lib," I say. "That may be true but I also saw you get your ass kicked. Is it really worth it? I mean, it's our last year here, let's try to get through it alive."

He stops and looks at me coldly. "Mauricio Gutiérrez, what happened to that fighting spirit from a few months ago? *You're* the one who came up with the idea in the first place."

I bow my head. "I know. But that was then, when Isaac was still around and you weren't a gay-bashing target."

"Oh, come on," Lib says. He sits up on the examination table. "You're going to let a little blood stop the movement?"

"The movement?" I ask. "Lib, will you listen to yourself? You're talking crazy. There *is* no movement, just one excitable little Goth queen who's running on the adrenaline rush of her first fight."

Lib shakes his head and puts the gauze back over his mouth.

"Look, Lib, I'm sorry. But I've got a different path to follow. I mean, *you* have a bright future ahead of you. You're the only one of the group who's going to get a first-rate education and I can see you going into law and becoming a politician or something. I mean, I can see you being like our next Gavin Newsom. Yeah, Mayor Liberace García of San Francisco. And Trini and I will cheer you on from your hometown turf and shit. We'll be your

Rigoberto González

Caliente, California constituency. We'll throw fundraisers at Las Cazuelas. We'll..."

My voice trails off into a tearful whimper.

"Hey," Lib says, softly.

I've got grief boogers clogging up my nostrils. "Sorry."

Lib hops off the examination table. "Now it's you who's talking silly. I don't understand why you're stopping yourself this way. The doors close up so quickly for you."

"And what am I suppose to do?" I almost shout. How do I explain to a guy like Lib who's expected to go onto bigger things that I don't have the same bright future? That I have to put my life on pause for the next three years. "I can't leave my father here alone after Mickey takes off for college. And what if Isaac comes back and doesn't find me here?"

"Oh, Maui," Trini says. He puts his arm around me. "You see? You keep trying to be everyone's safety net. And nobody's asking you. Your father didn't tell you not to go away to college. Isaac never told you to wait around for him. You're not being fair to yourself *or* to them."

I keep sniffling. I don't know what else to say. Lib's right, but there's nothing much I can do about it to change things. I've made my mind up. I'm going to stay in Caliente no matter how much it hurts, and I'm going to keep my father company until my turn comes to fly the coop. In the meantime, I just have to keep a low profile, and not embarrass my father by getting into sticky, public situations like this one.

Within a week of the incident at the club fair, Lib speeds through the school like a comet. He convinces his parents not to raise too much of a stink over the attack, and they agree, but only after the school principal allows Lib to do his thing. I know, they're too good to be true, Lib's parents, but indeed they're real, loyal to their convictions through and through, though they still wish he'd remove the piece of metal off his face and, frankly, so do I, if only for his safety. I sometimes help Lib put up flyers and sometimes even Trini joins in and we decorate his here-to-stay *The Mariposa Club: A Gay/Straight Alliance* signs with paint from the student activities office. But mostly we keep out of his way because he's a mean single-engine machine.

By the time Thanksgiving rolls around, Lib has organized a special rally with speakers coming in all the way from LA, but anyone who wants to attend has to bring a parent permission form, which produces mixed results. Parents call in to complain, making threats that they'll take their kids out of the high school and in the end the whole thing gets canceled because of "lack of interest."

But Mayor Lib (as he's become known) is unfazed. He even gets some attention from the local media and he milks it for all its worth.

"Hey," Mickey says to me as she sits in the living room, watching TV. "Lib's on the news again."

I look up from the dinner table, my textbooks spread open in front of me. Mickey raises the volume.

"I think it's important to take this issue to the community," he says into the microphone. He's taken to wearing a black blazer and tie, so now he looks like a Goth businessman. "Which is why I want to set up an informational booth at the mall during the Holiday Village Arts & Crafts Fair. What better time to demonstrate goodwill to *all* men. And women."

"Is he nuts?" I say. I can't imagine this is going to fly in a place like the Lame View Mall. We live in Caliente, not LA.

"Wow," Mickey says. "I for one am impressed. But I wouldn't worry too much about his safety. He's still just a kid, and then Celie will be at the mall, keeping an eye out."

Rigoberto González

I'm still uneasy about his plans. I'm going to have to take it up with him the next time I see him. At the very least I hope Celie will bring in those Goth bouncers from her party.

The Return of Isaac

The start of the Christmas shopping season makes even Lame View Mall not look so lame anymore with the hustle and bustle of credit card carriers buzzing around, everyone looking for a deal because times are tougher this year. The mall stays open late during this time of year, and my father has given me permission to put in some extra hours at the jewelry store, but only if I don't fall behind on my homework. Every day the holiday music blasts through the corridors, people passing by get carried away by the strong festive current, and Mr. Dutton wears an especially pleased smile on his face since his jewelry store attracts more than its share of bargain-seekers. With the increase of bodies huddled around the lighted display cases, the temperature rises inside the store. By the end of the night, Mr. Dutton and I are sweating like gym bunnies. And that's how we transition from late November into early December—soaking our clothes with perspiration. I feel the drops of sweat run down my back and collect at my waist, stopped by my cinched belt. Mr.

Dutton suffers through it in his coat and tie no matter how warm it gets.

Everyone seems happy, except for Lib, who's been denied permission to set up his booth among the "family-oriented" ones of the Holiday Village Arts & Crafts Fair. But he's not the one I'm worried about at the moment: Mr. Dutton's been feeling under the weather these last few weeks, and all this added holiday stress isn't helping any. But he's determined to tough it out and refuses to close the store early like he usually does when he's not feeling well.

"Maui, come translate for me, please," he calls out to me.

I excuse myself momentarily from a father and his young daughter. A Mexican lady wearing gold earrings stands next to Mr. Dutton. She looks like a serious shopper, so I put on my most professional demeanor to speak with her. From the corner of my eye I watch Mr. Dutton walk behind the display cases and take a seat on the only chair we keep around. He takes out a white handkerchief from his pocket and wipes his brow.

The Mexican lady isn't pleased that she has to deal with the kid and not the boss, so her tone remains unfriendly throughout the exchange. I keep looking over to Mr. Dutton.

A few minutes later, the Mexican lady leaves, not quite satisfied with the distracted attention I give her. I immediately turn to Mr. Dutton. "Are you okay, sir?"

He waves his white handkerchief at me. I accept that as a response and stay on task. The air in the store remains stale all evening as customer after customer enters. Every once in a while I'll catch a whiff of strong perfume or cologne and it makes my nose itch.

By closing time, Trini comes over to help out. She's been busy with her own responsibilities, keeping a close watch on Aunt Carmen, who seems to have taken a turn for the worse. She doesn't

Rigoberto González

say anything but I know how terrified she is of losing her aunt, of having to seek sanctuary at my house again.

"It smells in here," she says, covering her nose with her scarf.

"Tell me about it," I say. I start pulling down the security barriers. "Everyone just comes in to sweat!"

"Well, you might want to introduce Mr. Dutton to the box fan," Trini says. "This place needs some airing out. Pew!"

"I'm leaving now, Mr. Dutton!" I yell out, hoping Mr. Dutton will hear me in the back. No answer. "Mr. Dutton?"

"Maybe he left," Trini says. "Come on, let's roll."

I flash her a skeptical smirk. "I don't think he would leave without making sure I've locked the security barriers. Let me just make sure."

"Good grief, Maui. I need to get back by seven o'clock to make sure Aunt Carmen takes her pills before she passes out for the night. The last time I had to shove them down her throat with my finger. Not pleasant."

I shake my head. "Just give a second."

I duck under the low barriers and make my way to the back room. "Mr. D.?" I call out. "Mr. Dutton, are you okay?"

As soon as I open the door and catch sight of Mr. Dutton slumped over on the floor, I know he's not okay. I have no idea how many minutes pass or how many times I actually breathe the whole time I'm checking to see if he's alive, reaching for the phone to dial 911, yelling out to Trini to call Celie, waiting for the ambulance to show up and haul Mr. Dutton off to the hospital. All I know is that it's déjà vu when I finally find myself sitting in the hospital waiting room with the same bored receptionist behind her desk, sneaking calls on her cell.

"Maui," Papi calls out as soon as he comes in. I stand up and let him wrap his arm over my shoulder. "How are you doing?"

"Shaken up," I say, remembering Trini's own encounter with this type of crisis at Aunt Carmen's. "Where's Trini?"

"He called me at work," Papi says. "He can't leave Aunt Carmen alone tonight, she's a little delicate. And Mrs. Dutton?"

"Her neighbor brought her over," I say. "She's in there now with one of the girls."

"Terrible news," Papi says. "And he's so young to have a heart attack. But I guess one never knows."

"No," I say. This whole time I've been thinking about Isaac. How are we going to let him know? His cell has long-ago been disconnected. He should know that his father's in the hospital no matter *what* went on between them.

Jane, the oldest Dutton sister, walks into the waiting room.

"Hey, Jane," I say in the softest voice I can muster.

"How's your father, Jane?" my father asks.

"The doctor says he's stable," she says. "He just needs to rest."

"Thank, God," I say. "I knew he was over-exerting himself at the jewelry store."

"I called Isaac," Jane blurts out.

My body freezes. "What? You know how to reach him?"

Jane nods. Her hair is as blonde as Isaac's; her eyes just as blue. "I promised him I would only use it in case of an emergency. I wasn't allowed to tell anyone I had it."

I'm hurt that he couldn't trust me the same way, but I have to understand. "Is he coming? Where is he?"

"He's in LA and he's coming tonight," Jane says. "That's why I'm telling you. Mom and I need to go back home because we left my sisters alone, so we can't be here. But Mom said maybe you can stay so that he won't be alone when he arrives."

I look up at my father, who nods, catching on to the situation.

"I'll be at home if you need me, Maui," Papi says. "But be nice. It's not going to be easy for Isaac to deal with all of these things at once."

Rigoberto González

I nod. My father leaves the hospital. Fifteen minutes later Jane and Mrs. Dutton leave with their neighbor, Mrs. Dutton in tears. I walk up to the pay phones and call Lib.

"Hello?" Lib says.

"It's me."

"Maui, what happened? Celie came over with the news but she couldn't tell me much."

"Mr. Dutton had a heart attack," I say.

"Poor Mr. Dutton," Lib says. "Is he okay?"

"He just needs rest for now. But listen, that's not what I called to tell you."

After a short silence on the phone, after a brief moment of me staring at the pastel décor in the waiting room, Lib shouts, "Well?"

"Isaac's coming," I say.

"You're kidding me! Where the hell has he been?"

"In LA, apparently. Jane just broke the news."

"No shit. Are you okay?" Lib asks. I'm letting the pregnant pauses use up my time on the pay phone.

"No, yes—I don't know. I don't know what to think or say right now. It's all happening so fast. He's gone, and then he's back. I need to sit down."

"Wait, don't hang up! Damn, this is some heavy shit! What are you going to tell him?"

"I don't know. That I'm pissed. That I'm confused. I won't know until I actually see him. Maybe I'll just cry. I'll tell you later, okay? My time's running out. I have to go."

"Call me tonight!" Lib says. "No matter how late. And tell him that we miss him!"

"I will."

"Hugs, Maui!" Lib says, and then I hang up the phone.

I'm exhausted suddenly. Mr. Dutton's heart attack, Isaac's return—it's too much to take in one breath, so I close my eyes for a second and pretend that it's not me sitting anxiously in a hospital waiting room. I need to keep from succumbing to the fears that come so naturally in places like this—death, sickness, despair. I breathe out and release some of that anxiety back into the air.

I've never been good with the waiting game, especially because there isn't any kind of estimated time of arrival. There isn't even a *certainty* of an arrival. I sit facing the sliding door entrance, looking up each time I hear them open. After an hour or so of this boring exercise, I relax enough to get a soda, though I need to save my change to call my father later in the evening. And once I even make a weak attempt at doing homework, though I'm so distracted and tired at this point that I close the books and simply slump down on the uncomfortable seat. I get so zoned out that when I actually see someone walk in who looks like Isaac I don't even react, so sure that it isn't him. But then he makes eye contact and smiles and my stomach nearly explodes.

"Hey, Maui."

It's Isaac all right, but it still takes a moment for it to sink in. My body shakes as he comes close. It doesn't get any better when we actually embrace and it's as if it was all just a bad dream, this absence of Isaac's from my life the last few months.

"Hey," I finally manage to stutter.

"How's my father?" he asks. And I'm glad for this question. It will allow me to focus on the practical reason for his sudden appearance and not on the flurry of emotions beating inside me at the moment.

"Stable," I say. "I'm not sure they'll let you go in this late, though. Visiting hours are over."

"I know. I just asked," Isaac says. "But I wanted to come down tonight anyway. That way I can deal with my return first, with my father second."

Rigoberto González

"There are too many questions swimming in my head right now, Isaac," I say, sitting down. "I think my head's going to split open."

Isaac laughs. He reaches down and strokes my cheek with his hand.

"God, Isaac," I snap, moving away from him. "You think it's that easy for me to just slip back into the way things were before you took off without an explanation?"

"I knew you'd be mad. I don't blame you."

"Yeah, well, I blame *you*," I say. "How could you do that to us? We're your friends, remember?"

"I remember," Isaac says. "But it was easier to forget at that moment. Otherwise I wouldn't have been able to leave. And I needed to get out of here."

"Shithead," I say. My eyes well up with tears and I wipe them off quickly. This time when Isaac reaches over to stroke my cheek I let him.

"Maybe if you explain to the nurse that you came all this way, she'll let you in to see your father," I say, trying to shift Isaac's attention away from me.

"We should let him rest. I'll be back here tomorrow morning."

After a brief pause I ask, "Then what do we do now?"

"Well, I've still got my Honda. You still got enough energy in you to hear me babble and apologize a thousand times?"

It almost feels like the old days with me riding shotgun as Isaac weaves in and out of the streets of the Caliente Valley. We pass the high school, though it's still the same old "institution of lesser learning," but Isaac says it looks different to him. I guess it would to someone who hasn't attended classes in almost three months. Isaac, I suddenly realize, is our very own high school drop-out. We circle the entire campus for good measure, and then we cruise down the main avenue to trigger memories of all the other times we did that, drive without urgency because all we had was time.

We don't even discuss it, but we finally make our way to the Lame View Mall, where we park at the old spot.

"Celie still keeping order?" he asks.

"You know it," I say. "And Lib, geez, you should see him now. He's like the big man on campus and even got his lip pierced."

"No kidding?" Isaac says.

"Trini?"

"The same," I say, aware that we're just delaying the serious talk, so I get right to it though it comes out sounding a little sappy. "We all miss you, Isaac. Are you coming back?"

"Well, I'm not coming back to school, if that's what you mean," he says. "I have a new life now in LA. I have a job and I'm, umm, actually seeing someone."

My eyes widen. "Serious? You have a boyfriend? A *real* boy-friend?"

Isaac laughs. I realize then that indeed he has changed—he's grown up, leaving the rest of us behind in our adolescent dramas. We're facing the cars driving on the avenue, same as we always did. But Isaac and I are no longer moving through the world at the same pace. This is still my present. This is Isaac's past.

"What about your father?" I ask.

"I don't know. I don't think that even a heart attack is going to amend his ways. I mean, *I'm* not going to change, I'll always be gay."

"But he *has* changed a little," I say. "He even lets Trini into the store now."

"Trini's not his son."

He's right. Mr. Dutton doesn't have to live with Trini and doesn't have to see him for more than a few minutes a day. Trini isn't going to take over the store and carry on the reputation of the family business.

Rigoberto González

"I didn't realize it was that bad for you," I say, finally.

"It was worse at home," Isaac says. "A lot of yelling, throwing my things out the window he thought were gay, like my tank tops and my Greek mythology textbook."

"You're kidding."

Isaac shakes his head. "And that time we got suspended for ditching school, he grabbed a handful of hair right out of my head. It was his excuse to get at me for everything else he found offensive."

I couldn't reconcile this portrait of Mr. Dutton with the person I had grown to respect. But then I thought about Trini and the people that had abused her. I bet their public faces were different also. We sit in the quiet for a while, unable to continue this conversation. It's getting too painful.

"So what's his name?" I say, trying to break the silence with a new subject.

"Armando," Isaac says. I look at him. "You know I've always had a thing for Latinos."

I punch him in the arm and we have a laugh finally.

"How did you meet him?" I ask.

"Armando owns a clothing store on Sunset Boulevard. I was living in my car the first few days and I was lucky enough to walk into his shop, looking for a something clean to wear. I had to find a way to survive, Maui, so I let things run their course: a friendship, an employment, and eventually more than that. A relationship.."

"That easy?" I say.

"Of course not," Isaac says. "At one point I thought I was going to—"

"Going to what?"

"You know," Isaac says. "End it before it got too desperate. So I owe a lot to Armando. Even if he's a little difficult sometimes."

"What do you mean?"

The Mariposa Club

"Nothing," Isaac says, looking away. "Forget I said that."

"What? Tell me." I can only imagine the worse. "I thought we could tell each other anything."

Isaac shakes his head. "Look, Armando's taking care of me. He saved my life. I feel lucky, you know. It could've ended badly for me. Drugs, prostitution. Or worse."

"Geez" I say, and then feel stupid for blurting out such a dopey reaction.

"Hey, Maui. I want to thank you for looking out for my father."

"Well, that's what I do best," I say with a bit of sarcasm. "Look after fathers."

After a few seconds of silence Isaac reaches over and holds my hand. I'm grateful for the touch.

"Why didn't you trust me to keep your new number a secret?" I say finally.

"Because I didn't want to put you in the difficult situation of lying," Isaac says.

"But you trusted your sister," I say.

"That's because I promised her money," Isaac says. "And she's my annoying little sister—she's supposed to be a big fat liar."

We break out laughing again.

"Don't you wish, though, that it was like it used to be? Just the Fierce Foursome wreaking havoc at the Queer Planter?"

Isaac lets go of my hand and relaxes his head over the headrest.

"Did I say something wrong?" I ask.

"Listen, Maui," Isaac says, facing me. "I made a choice, not a mistake. I left school, messed up my future, I'm sure, but I'm much happier."

"But it's not too late to pick up where you left off," I say. "You've only been gone a few months."

Rigoberto González

Isaac shakes his head. "It's not as simple as that, Maui. I'm in a different place now. The best I can do is stick around to help out at the store until my father gets well again. That's assuming he'll even let me. And then I need to get back to my new life. Armando's waiting for me."

My eyes start to water. "No, I guess I don't understand. I thought we were going to be friends for life."

Isaac leans over to hug me. "Nothing's for life, Maui. You know that more than anyone."

And I know it's true. Nothing's for life. Everything's temporary. Anything can vanish without notice.

"You want to put Cyndi on and then we can speed down the avenue to your house?" Isaac asks.

"No, no music," I say. "Let's just drive slowly. I'm in no hurry."

I don't ask any more questions. I'm still curious about so many things in Isaac's new life, but I've received all the important answers. He's only here for a visit. By Christmas, he's gone. But he'll be in touch—"Promise."

Maddy

Isaac's return doesn't change the way the lives of those he left behind are lived. Lib continues with his campaign, and has been getting visits from Ivy League school recruiters, which pleases Boozely no end. He even got a scholarship handed to him by an LGBT organization in Palm Springs, so for the first time ever he got to make a trip to the city without wearing any see-through clothing.

Trini has been looking into cosmetology school and is delighted to find out there's a local license-granting facility in the valley. Aunt Carmen's been through a few health scares but she always manages to bounce back. "She's not ready to take her final bow, that's for sure," Trini says.

As for me, I'm happy to have Isaac around again. Mr. Dutton has agreed to let Isaac keep Joyería Dutton open part-time so it's just the two of us in the afternoons and on weekends while Mr. Dutton stays at home recovering, anxious to get back to work. It's not clear if the two of them have reconciled, but they've been civil on the phone this whole time whenever Isaac calls him from the store when he has a question.

The mall's still going strong and ever since the ambulance came to pick up Mr. Dutton, nothing exciting has happened. The only activity is Celie chasing out Los Calis from the premises.

About the only annoying thing is that when Isaac drives me home in the evenings, Armando always calls and Isaac spends the entire drive assuring him that everything's fine, that he misses him too, and that he can't wait to get back. I don't blame Armando. I know what it's like to lose Isaac.

"Sorry about that," Isaac says as soon as he coaxes his boyfriend off the phone. By that point we're already on my street.

"No worries," I say.

"God, I've been dying for a cigarette," Isaac says. "But I promised Armando I'd quit."

I want to roll my eyes but resist. There he is again: Armando.

"Sorry," Isaac says. "I'm being annoying, aren't I?"

"Slightly," I confess. "But I understand. I think I'm going to be the same whenever I get my first boyfriend."

Isaac laughs. "It'll be something to look forward to."

We pull up to the driveway and Isaac parks the car. This has become our nightly goodbye ritual, an echo of all the times we have sat at the parking lot of Lame View Mall, just talking. The car is the only privacy we can get, especially for someone like Isaac who has a house full of nosy little sisters.

"Whose car is that?" Isaac asks, pointing at a blue Corolla in the driveway.

I shrug my shoulders. "Maybe a friend of Mickey's. She's all excited about transferring to a university next fall."

"I'm happy for her," Isaac says. "And how about you?"

I purse my lips. "Let's not go there right now."

"Oh," Isaac says. "What's going on?"

I'm not ready to get into this. "Nothing," I say.

Rigoberto González

"Nothing?" Isaac asks. "Since when are telling each other 'nothing'?"

"Since you left," I snap and immediately regret it.

He remains speechless for a few seconds. "I guess I deserved that," he says.

"No," I say. "You didn't. I'm sorry that slipped out like that."

Isaac keeps quiet and doesn't pry any further, but I feel bad enough about it that I go ahead and tell him about Mickey's expectations of me, about our agreement. But that only manages to make me agitated all over again.

"That doesn't seem fair," Isaac says.

"It sucks," I say. "But *she* stayed behind two years and now it's my turn."

"And what does your father want?" Isaac says.

"Does it matter? Do the wishes of our parents really change what we do or don't do?" I feel the words making knots in my throat.

Isaac's eyes narrow. "Wow, Maui. You're really shooting to kill tonight. Is there anything else you need to get off your chest before I throw you out of my car?"

"I think I'm done, boss," I say, out of breath. "I'll see you at work tomorrow."

I scamper out of the car and slam the door closed.

"Maui," Isaac calls out. "Let's not leave things like this, okay?"

But his pleas are useless. I'm too pissed off and I know I can't keep having a conversation with him without other ugly words getting into the mix. He knows me well enough that he simply turns the ignition and takes off. Nothing's going to get resolved in two seconds. We'll just have to deal with this tomorrow, when I've had the night to calm down.

I open the door, expecting to simply walk in, fix a snack and go to my room, but I'm met instead by the sight of Mickey in her bathrobe and curlers. Sitting next to her is Maddy in tears.

The Mariposa Club

"What's going on?" I ask. I'm suddenly terrified that something has happened to Sheriff Johnson.

"Never mind, Maui," Mickey says. "We need some privacy."

"Well, let me grab a fruit or something and I'll go to my room."

Mickey's eyes are fixed on me as I drag my feet from the door to the kitchen through the living room and to my room, where I slowly close my door, but leave it ajar. Just like Isaac has four nosy little sisters at home, Mickey has one nosy little brother. But I can't resist. The last time Maddy ever made her way down here was when Mickey had to babysit her.

"It's all up to you, Maddy," Mickey says. "It's your body. Your choice."

Maddy breaks down sobbing. "But I love Walter, and I want him to help me raise our baby."

"I understand," Mickey says, patiently. "But you're both all of eighteen. Neither of you has jobs, and raising a child is costly."

"I'm keeping this baby," Maddy says with conviction. "This baby needs a mama the way I always needed a mama." My face flushes. I know exactly what she means.

"I'm not saying you shouldn't keep the baby. But do you think your father will help out?"

"No, he won't. He's going to kill me," Maddy says.

"Don't be silly. He loves you. In any case you're going to have to tell him. It's not like it's something you can keep a secret."

"I know it's not," Maddy says. Her voice is gentle. I had forgotten it could be that way. "Will you be here to help me?"

"As long as I'm able to," Mickey says. "You're like my little sister, Maddy. And then, after I'm gone, Maui can help. He'll still be around. He can be the new babysitter and keep the tradition alive."

"WHAT?!" I yell out.

Rigoberto González

"Maui, you little jerk!" Mickey yells back. "You were eavesdropping on a personal conversation!"

I rush out of my room. "Well, if you're going to get me involved I have every right to know."

"Maui, not now," Mickey says.

"Do you want me to break his bones, Mickey?" Maddy offers between sobs.

Mickey raises her hands. "No, thank you, Maddy. Let me take care of this. Maui, go to your room!"

"You can't send me to my room," I say.

"Yes, I can," Mickey says. "And I can still get the belt, too."

I'm in disbelief. The belt is the age-old threat that was never actually executed, but it used to work—back when I was five.

"You can't boss me around like that, Mickey," I protest, getting loud. "And stop trying to run my life also. I have my *own* plans for the future."

"We've been through this, Maui," Mickey says, pursing her lips. She stands up and tries to shove me out of the living room. "It's not about what *I* want. It's about what's best for Papi. Now go to your room, I want to finish talking with Maddy."

I resist. "What? Are you going to tell her what to do also?" I turn to Maddy. "Be careful what you wish for."

"That's *it*!" Mickey says, stomping her foot. "Get out! Get out, right now before I do something I'll really regret!"

"Don't you threaten me, sister," I say.

But I have indeed pushed Mickey to the limit and she grabs me by the shirt. I try to pull her hold off me but lose my balance and then we both tumble down to the floor.

"Get off me!" I say.

And then Maddy stands over us and screams: "I can't believe you two!"

Mickey and I freeze.

The Mariposa Club

Maddy takes a deep breath and lets us have it: "I'm pregnant and scared shitless, so I come over here to seek help from my second family and you all start bickering about your own messes! You two are the most selfish, self-centered people I have ever seen! Mrs. Gutiérrez would be so embarrassed to see you now, rolling on the floor like a pair of dogs fighting over the same piece of trash. I'm out of here."

Mickey and I quickly jump to our feet. I'm holding one of her baby blue hair curlers in my hand.

"Maddy, wait!" Mickey calls out. "Please, don't go. We're sorry."

Mickey elbows me in the ribs. "Yeah," I say. "Sorry."

I know this would not be enough to convince anyone, especially not Maddy, but tonight Maddy has no choice. She's in a bind and she needs to talk things through. Without further discussion, the three of us sit together in the living room.

"Can I make some tea or something?" I offer.

"I'll take a glass of water," Maddy says. Mickey nods at me to comply.

As I scare up some ice from the freezer, Maddy sighs.

"What else am I going to do anyway," she says. "It's not like I was going to college or anything. I'm barely getting through."

"That's not the point," Mickey says. "Responsibilities are responsibilities, whether or not you're a dishwasher or a lawyer. What you and Walter need to do is make a plan."

"But Walter *is* college material," Maddy says.

I bring Maddy the glass of water. I guess I'm stunned by this revelation most of all. Walter never seemed like the college-type at all. One never knows.

"So is he or isn't he going to be part of the baby's life?" Mickey asks.

Maddy starts to cry again. "I don't know. Right now he's as scared shitless as I am."

Rigoberto González

"Then don't make any big decisions just yet," Mickey says. "Just have some options ready for whatever comes your way. You're an adult now, Maddy. You need to start thinking like one."

Except for that loose strand of hair on the side of her head, the one I accidentally pulled out in our two-second cat fight, Mickey actually looks and sounds very mature. Maddy nods and Mickey inches in a little closer to hug her. I can't help but let a tear drop as well.

"What do you have to cry about?" Maddy says.

"I don't know," I say, wiping away my tear, though I'm thinking about Isaac. "I guess I'm happy for you and sad for you. These things seem to come hand in hand all the time. Growing up is hard, isn't it?"

A knock at the door disrupts the moment of reflection. I walk over and take a peek through the peephole.

"It's Snake!" I shriek. "I mean, Walter."

"Oh, my God," Mickey says. "I can't let a man see me like this." She rushes out of the living room with her hands over her hair curlers.

"Do I let him in?" I ask Maddy.

"Go ahead," she says. "I can handle it."

I open the door. The second shock is that Snake—Walter, that is—stands there looking more cleaned up than I've ever seen him.

"Hey," I say, trying to play it cool.

"Is Maddy here?" he asks. His question sounds more like a plea. I open the door wider so that he can see her sitting on the couch.

"Maddy," Snake says. "I've been texting you all evening."

Maddy reaches into her purse and takes out her phone. "Oh," she says. "It was off."

"That doesn't matter," Snake says. "I found you anyway. I figured you might come this way."

The Mariposa Club

After an awkward silence I realize that I'm a spare wheel here so I excuse myself, only to bump into Mickey eavesdropping around the corner.

"Shhh," she says.

"Oh, so listening to other people's conversations is fine when you do it?" I say, and I take my place just behind her.

"Well, what do you want?" Maddy asks in a severe tone. She crosses her arms.

"Maddy, please," Snake says. "Can we go somewhere else to talk?"

"I'm staying right here. If you got something to say, spit it out."

"I came to say I'm sorry."

"Sorry about being such a chickenshit or sorry I got pregnant?"

"About being a chickenshit," Snake says.

"And what are we going to do about the baby?"

Snake scratches his head. "Well, we can get married. I don't want my child to grow up a bastard like I did."

"Get married?" Maddy gasps.

Mickey and I grab each other.

"But I don't have an engagement ring, yet," he adds.

"Walter Eugene Simmons, when did you make up your mind about us getting married, anyway, this morning?"

"Eugene?" I whisper.

"Actually, just right now, as soon as I saw your car parked in the driveway. That's why I don't have a ring."

"I can get them a deal at Dutton's," I whisper to Mickey, who elbows me.

A lengthy silence follows before Maddy eventually uncrosses her arms, sighs in relief and speaks up again. "There's still a lot we need to talk about, Walter, but I accept. And nothing's a done deal until you meet my father. And until I get an engagement ring on this finger."

Rigoberto González

"You got it, Maddy," Snake says.

"Oh, Walter," Maddy cries out between sniffles. A lengthy silence follows.

"Gross," I say. "They're making out on the couch. I eat popcorn there."

"Maui," Mickey says, looking back at me. "Never mind."

Unwanted Suitors

With the weekend upon us, and this being the last haul before Christmas break, Isaac started picking me up at school instead of waiting to see if Trini could get me to the mall fast enough. Sometimes Trini got anxious and had to stop in and see Aunt Carmen first, which cut into the time it took for me to get to work and sometimes even more if Aunt Carmen needed something special—like a diaper change. At fifteen, Jane had started her training, so she was able to hold fort at the jewelry store while Isaac came to pick me up. The trip was quick, no more than ten minutes: zoom into the school parking lot, zoom out to the mall. Cyndi Lauper on the CD player.

By the time we walk into the mall, the crowd at Dutton's is antsy for attention. Isaac and I hit the floor running.

"May I help you?" I ask a customer, as I slide my backpack off my shoulder.

"I'd like to see that piece there, with the pearl," the customer says.

Isaac has a brief exchange with Jane, who seems to be taking a liking to the role. Other girls her age might be upset that their social life has been compromised but not Jane—she likes money. Making it and spending it.

"Maui," Jane says. "There was a guy here earlier looking for you?"

"Lib?" I ask.

"No, not the Dracula dude," she says. "The handsome one. Is it your boyfriend?"

I pucker my lips and do a baby imitation of Jane: "*Is it your boyfriend?* No, it's not my boyfriend, and it's also none of your beeswax, Snoopy."

"K-i-s-s-i-n-g," Jane chants as she moves on to a customer.

I don't have too much time to wonder who this mysterious caller is because I see him approaching. It's David. He cuts through the crowd and walks directly up to me.

"Hello," he says. "Busy afternoon?"

"How may I help you, sir," I say, trying to keep calm and composed, though today there's something a little bit attractive about David. Maybe it's the whole "older boyfriend" thing that worked out for Isaac. But that's Isaac. I'm Maui, Passion Flower, the seventeen-year-old virgin.

"I love it when you call me that," David says. He leans in to wink at me.

I shudder. I'm actually able to shudder in this warm, crowded jewelry store.

"Are you here to find your stud?" I ask.

"You could say that," David says.

I shudder again. I'm not made for this. This is Trini's territory—she's always good with the witty comebacks, the double entendres.

Rigoberto González

"If you follow me over here," I say, trying to pretend I don't hear what he's really saying. "You'll find a good selection of sizes in gold and silver."

David cuts through the crowd until he's facing me over the display case. I pull out the exhibit to give him a closer look.

"Well, you tell me," David says. He turns his head to show me his ear. "Can you find a match for me?"

My hands are shaking as I calculate a potential size match and then pull out a stud to bring it up to his ear. And just as I feared, David seizes the opportunity to bring his hand up as well to hold mine. I pull my hand away, dropping the stud. It hits the glass and bounces down to the floor on my side.

"I'm so sorry," he says. "Do I make you nervous? There's nothing to be nervous about. I don't bite. Not the first time."

"Listen," I say, firmly. "I'm going to ask you to leave."

David looks surprised by my change in tone, but it also seems to excite him. "Oh, really?" he says. "Are you telling me you don't like me?"

I stand there without responding.

"Not even a little?"

I refuse to speak. And to make matters worse, Jane comes over.

"That's the guy," Jane says. "Are you his boyfriend?" she asks David.

David chuckles. "Well, I'd like to be"

"Ooh," Jane says. "Hey, Isaac!"

"Jane," I say. "Quit it."

"Isaac!" Jane persists. "Maui's got a man! Maui's got a man!"

People in the jewelry store start to turn around. Finally Isaac comes over and flicks his finger on Jane's head.

"How old are you, ten?" he says to Jane. "Get to work or I'm cutting your pay."

The Mariposa Club

Begrudgingly, Jane steps away. I turn to Isaac and give him the "help me out" look.

Isaac turns to David, who looks amused by the spectacle. "May I help you?" Isaac asks.

"I'm being taken care of, thank you," David says. "I'll take a pair of these." He points to the stud. The other pair is somewhere near my feet.

I duck down to retrieve it. I let out a deep sigh.

"You find it?" Isaac asks.

"I know it's here somewhere."

"Perhaps I should come back another time," David says. And he casually walks as I crouch on the rug, feeling for the fallen stud.

"Just forget about it," Isaac says, and then his tone changes when a customer approaches. "Yes, how may I help you? Hoops? Yes."

I get up and smooth out my shirt and in seconds I'm giving my undivided attention to another customer.

Two hours later I take my break. Trini and Lib agree to come by and help out at the jewelry store since Isaac doesn't want to overexert Jane. (That is, he wants her out his hair sooner than later.) The girls meet me at the food court.

"He's a different Isaac, that's for sure," Lib says. All three of us sit at a distance, watching.

"Moodier, too," Trini says. "What's street life done to him? He's come back as cold as Cruella."

"Well, let's not exaggerate," I say. "He's just going through a lot. His father, the store, that boyfriend of his that keeps calling like a maniac."

"Separation issues," Trini says. "I've been reading about it in *Out* magazine."

"Well, let's catch up, girls," I say. "I feel like it's been forever since we've hung out."

Rigoberto González

"True that," Trini says. "But Aunt Carmen's been a bit of a pill, lately. She's not liking that new diet the doctor put her on in order to fatten her up a bit. She's worried about her figure. And I tell her, 'Hon, you a stick figure, that's what *you* are at the moment. Now eat!'"

"Okay," Lib says. "Anyway, I'm—"

Trini swats at him. "I'm not finished giving my report yet, Miss Commercial Interruption."

Lib purses his lips. "Go on, then."

"Thank you," Trini says, indignant. "So David finally called."

"What?" I say.

Trini's eye flutter. "Yes, you know, Davy Wavy?"

"Is that why he's here today?" I ask.

"He *is*?" Trini looks around. "Where? He didn't tell me he was going to be here. Oh, Maui, you party pooper, you spoiled the surprise!"

Lib rolls his eyes.

"So he called to chat, and we chatted," Trini says. "We talked about school, about my friends, what kind of music I liked. You know, the usual stuff."

"That's it?" I say.

"Well, we're taking it slow," Trini says. "Relationships don't just happen, you know. I'm a lady! I'm not going to take off my petticoat for the first gentleman caller who comes riding up in a fancy carriage. I've got standards."

"She's got standards," Lib says, raising his eyebrows.

"And what about you, Candidate Candy Cane? What do you have to report from campaign headquarters?" Trini asks.

Lib straightens his back and takes a deep breath. "Well, it's sort of like a secret plan at the moment," he says. "And I don't want to get you girls into trouble so I can't reveal all the details. But let me just say that The Mariposa Club: A Gay/Straight Alliance will be

The Mariposa Club

fabulously represented at the Holiday Village Arts & Crafts Fair this weekend."

"You got permission to put a booth up? That's great!" I say.

"Well, not exactly."

"What do you mean, 'not exactly'?" I say, expressing concern.

Just then, Jane comes bouncing over. "Hello, girlfriends!" she says.

"Hi, June," Trini says.

"It's Jane," she replies with emphasis.

"That's what I said. June."

Jane smacks her lips. "Whatever, Trannie" she says.

"Trini," Trini says, firmly.

"That's what I said," Jane says. She then turns to me. "Maui, Isaac needs you. Armando just drove down from LA."

"Armando?" I say.

The three of us jump off our seats and can't get to the jewelry store fast enough.

"Oh, my God, we're going to meet the famous Armando!" Lib says.

"And me without time for a touch-up!" Trini says.

"Don't worry about *me*!" I hear Jane call out behind us.

We bump into each other when we finally stop just short of entering the store. Even through the crowd of bobbing heads in the way it's clear to see Isaac floating like he's got wings on his feet as he shuffles behind the display cases. All the while Armando stands with his arms crossed, his shoulder against the wall, watching.

"He looks so...old," Lib says.

Trini gives him the head-to-toe inspection. "He must be like, in his forties."

"He's like, as old as my father," I add.

But I have to admit, Armando isn't really all that bad-looking. He's more like Sheriff Johnson than Mr. Gutiérrez—no offense,

Rigoberto González

Papi—with a muscular upper body and narrow hips. But his face isn't smooth or preserved. It looks weathered and leathery, as if he has spent too much time baking on the beach.

The three of us make our way to the back.

"Hey, Maui," Isaac says. "Thank God you're back. Jane was driving us nutty with all her questions. This is Armando, by the way."

Armando nods his head. The silent, stoic type, I think, until I notice him looking at us up and down, scrutinizing Isaac's territory. He keeps coming back to me. It is I, he has decided, who is the threat. I can feel the hostile stare-down all over.

"We've heard so much about you," Trini finally says, breaking the awkward silent exchange. "I'm Trini. This is Lib. And that's Maui. And you're *divine!*"

This makes Armando break into a smile, and suddenly his face changes again and it looks friendly, kind—the kind of person I'm glad is watching over my best friend.

Until closing time, Isaac and I take care of business while Lib and Trini take turns keeping Armando company. And since it's Friday night, we decide to be the gracious hostesses and take Isaac's big city boyfriend to the only establishment in our small podunk town that's not going to embarrass us: Las Cazuelas.

Enough time has passed since the eventful night of the Latino Chamber of Commerce Annual Fundraising Banquet that we're comfortable stepping into the restaurant without getting the raised eyebrows from the employees. Yolanda the hostess seats our party of five in a large table at the corner and Armando orders a beer. The rest of us, noticeably underage, ask for soft drinks, except for Trini, who orders a "virgin" margarita.

"Maui's father manages this place," Isaac says. "Isn't it awesome?"

The Mariposa Club

"It's keeping it real, that's for sure," Armando says, and I can't help but feel offended because Armando is a man of the world. He's seen bigger, better, and probably more upscale Mexican restaurants.

"So, Armando," Trini says. "Tell us about your line of business. Tell us about your clothing store slash runaway refuge."

"Trini, that's so rude!" Lib says. Isaac looks mortified, but I'm secretly reveling in Trini's uncontrollable big-mouth antics. Lib turns to Armando. "We have to apologize on behalf of our friend, Armando. It's all those chemicals she puts on her face."

"That's all right," Armando says. "It's all in fun. Right, Trini?"

"Right, Armando," Trini says. "Oh, goodie, my margarita!"

"May I take your orders?" the server asks.

"Well, I'm a little low on funds," Trini says. "Maui, do you want to split a plate?"

"Hey, who am I going to split with?" Lib says.

"I'm not splitting with your fat ass," Trini says. "You end up eating more than your share."

"Then, why don't we just order appetizers," I suggest.

"It's on me, guys," Armando says.

"Well, in that case, I'll have the fajitas," Lib says.

"That's what *I* wanted," Trini says.

"Guys," Isaac jumps in, his face flushed. "I'm sure there are enough fajitas to go around. Now can we please make our orders so that we can eat?"

We order food, sip on our drinks and then, to Isaac's chagrin, Trini and Lib attack the tortilla chip basket when it's placed at the center of the table. Armando looks on amused.

The conversation is mostly chit-chat, mostly Trini hogging up the attention, which no one seems to mind, especially not me. I want to fade in the background tonight. Armando takes it in stride, moving quickly into his second beer, then his third. But

Rigoberto González

once Trini starts to stuff her face with steak and beans, Armando seizes on the moment of temporary silence to address me.

"So, Maui," he says. "You've been a little quiet. What's on your mind?"

Trini smiles. "Sex, probably. He's as virginal as my margarita."

"Don't talk with your mouth full," Lib says, talking with his mouth full.

I blush. "Oh, nothing. I'm just a little tired."

"It's hard to tell on such a pretty face," Armando says.

Everyone stops chewing and all eyes turn to me, including Isaac, whose eyes widen with concern.

"Isaac told me you were a good-looking boy. But I didn't realize how good looking until tonight."

The table goes completely silent now and suddenly the Mexican music coming in through the speakers above us sounds a little louder.

"Anything else I can get for you?" the server asks, surprising us.

"I'll have another beer," Armando says.

"You're driving, Armando," Isaac says. "I think you should—"

"I'll have that beer," Armando repeats his order. "Thank you."

The server nods and walks away.

Lib and Trini lock eyes and I simply sit there, waiting for Armando to make the next move.

"It's hard for me to believe you and Isaac never..." Armando lets us fill in the blank by moving his index and middle fingers back and forth in the air. "Or have you?"

"That's *enough*, Armando," Isaac says.

The force of Isaac's voice sobers Armando up a bit. He turns to me and says, "I'm sorry, Maui. I didn't mean to get personal. I'm a little tipsy, that's all."

"Maybe we should get a little fresh air," Isaac says. He stands up.

The Mariposa Club

"Yes," Armando says, following his lead. "That sounds like a good idea. I don't need that beer anyway. Well, guys, it's been a pleasure meeting all of you. Have a good night." He takes out his wallet and drops a one hundred dollar bill on the table.

"Good night," Trini and Lib say in unison. I stay quiet.

As soon as they leave, Trini and Lib lean in.

"Oh. My. Goddess," Lib says. "What was that all about?"

"Oh, that's easy," Trini says. "Armando thinks Maui's gotten what he hasn't."

"Do you really believe that?" Lib says. "That they haven't had sex."

"So says Isaac," Trini says, scooping up a spoonful of beans. "But until tonight I didn't believe it."

"Girls," I say. "Let's just drop it, okay? It's none of our business. Besides, that's not what's pissing me off."

The server comes back with a beer balanced on a serving tray.

"You can take that back," Trini says. "Our sloppy drinker just left."

The server smiles and goes away.

"What are you talking about?" Lib asks.

I sigh. "Nothing."

"Oh, come on," Trini pleads. "Sharing is caring."

"Nothing," I repeat. "I just thought it was kind of shitty that Isaac seemed embarrassed by us, that's all."

Lib looks confused. "I didn't notice anything."

"No," I say. "You were too busy fighting Trini for the tortilla chips."

"Well, that's who we are," Trini says. "We're still high school students without credit cards or disposable income. So what, the whole world has to change just because Isaac has a sugar daddy?"

"He's not a sugar daddy," Lib says.

Rigoberto González

Trini rolls her eyes "Bitch, please. Once Isaac turns eighteen he's also going to be his ho."

"Trini, that's nasty," I say. "This is our friend we're talking about."

"Our friend who's getting 'looked after' by a man twice his age," Trini says. "In my dictionary that means: ho."

"This from the girl who's got the hots for Davy Wavy?" Lib says.

"That's different," Trini says. "David and I have something special going."

"Do tell," Lib says, making eye contact with me. He takes a sip of his drink through his mischievous grin.

"David's a gentleman," Trini says. "He's classy, not tacky like this old insecure bitch. He *knows* how to make a girl feel like a lady. He's respectful and courteous. He's a dreamer, a man of the world who never forgets his manners."

Lib snorts. "Well if he's all that then why does he keep sniffing around the jewelry store in search of some Maui tail?"

I drop my fork. Trini turns to me.

"What's Hogatha talking about?" Trini says.

"Tell her, Maui. Tell this silly sally stick that her gentleman makes more calls to you than to her."

Trini straightens her back. "Well, this explains why David keeps bringing you up," she says, banging her fist on the table. "You've been sneaking around with my man behind my back!"

"Trini," I say. "No, you've got it all wrong."

"Trust your girlfriend to give you multiple stabs in the back," Trini says as she rises from her chair. "And that's what you were doing here tonight, wasn't it? Doing your innocent pretty boy act to get Armando's attention? I'm on to you, you two-faced temptress. It's because of easy tricks like you that the rest of us have to work ten times as hard just to keep a man!"

The Mariposa Club

"Good grief," Lib says. "Sit down, you're going to get us kicked out again."

Just then my father comes over to greet us.

"Hey, Maui. Hey, guys," Papi says. "I heard you were here tonight. How are things?"

"Oh, things are well, Mr. Gutiérrez," Trini says as she steps back and pushes her chair in. "As usual, the service is good, the food is hot and the clientele is *cold*. Good night, sir. I think these two are going to need a ride home. Me and Paulina Rubio are out of here." Trini snaps her fingers.

"All righty, then," my father says as soon as Trini stomps out of the restaurant. "You kids want to take some of these leftovers?"

Rigoberto González

About the Future

We drop Lib off in front of his family's unit at the housing project. Since it's Friday night the neighborhood is in full swing with loud car speakers and stereos blaring out through the apartment windows playing everything from Reggaetón to Juan Gabriel to old school banda music my father identifies as Cornelia Reyna.

"This is fun," he says, as we drive past another unit. "That's a little more modern. Who is that?"

I listen closely to the soft ballad. "Maná," I say. "They're still popular."

"I bet you don't know who *that* is," my father challenges me when we pass the next unit.

I smile. "That's Mercedes Sosa. We play her for Aunt Carmen. How about this one?"

"Lila Downs," my father says. "We have her CDs at the restaurant."

I'm loving this intimate moment with my father. I don't remember having many with him because I was such a mama's boy and preferred to stay close to Mami. But tonight it feels comfortable and natural, this father-son bonding that took shape all on its own. It's the kind of memory-making that will be all the sweeter because it was unplanned and unforced.

As we drive out of the projects the party ends and we're back on the quieter avenues of the streets. For all the times that I gripe about this little town, I have to confess it looks beautiful by car because cars mean safety, moving along, passing through and a way out.

"Isn't it exciting about Mickey?" Papi says. "Though I'm secretly glad she chose to transfer to Riverside. It's only an hour away. Close enough."

"Yes," I say. "She says she eventually wants to be a lawyer. I can see that. She can certainly argue."

Papi laughs. "That she can."

We drive past a few more streets before Papi finally breaks the silence. "And you?" he asks.

"Me what?"

"What do you want to do with your life?" he asks.

I look at my father from the corner of my eye. He's been working those late shifts all these years and it's taken a toll on his body. He's thinner than ever.

"I don't know, yet," I say. "I may need a few more years to think about it."

"A few more years?" he says. "And what are you going to do during those years? You'll be out of high school, you'll be eighteen. I hope you're thinking beyond a career at Mr. Dutton's. It's an honorable profession, of course, but I always thought you were made for something bigger."

I stay quiet although I'm dying to confess that the first thing I want to do after high school is leave Caliente. But I'm not sure

Rigoberto González

what this conversation is all about. Does he want me to confirm that I won't leave him or is he really serious about letting me make my own choice?

"What are some of your interests, Maui?" my father persists. "Medicine, business, education, the arts? Maybe law, like your sister?"

This conversation's making me feel awkward. Besides that I'm slightly bugged that my father has no idea what my interests are, I'm not really good about discussing my future plans. I always thought I'd just go to college. That's it. I figured that it would be *at* college where I'd discover what I was meant to do beyond my days of higher learning.

I remember last year, while we were getting the low-down on the SAT and the ACT and that ten-minute meeting with the school counselor that passed for academic advisement, I was told flat-out that I should pursue a profession in teaching literature because my essays were, according to my English teachers, "exceptional." But even if I do have a knack for words, I can't picture myself boring the hell out of students like Mr. Doze. No way. But that's the only thing I have to offer my father right now, so I blurt it out.

"I guess I wouldn't mind being an English teacher some day."

"You have to do more than 'not mind it,' Maui," my father says. "You have to be passionate about it. What are you passionate about?"

I'm stumped. What *is* the answer to this question? I guess I haven't really thought about it in terms of a passion. "I'm passionate about my family, my friends," I finally say, knowing that I'm missing his point.

"But beyond that, Maui," he says. "Are you passionate about politics like Lib or about fashion or beauty or whatever it is that Trini's passionate about?"

We're now moving at a slightly more urgent speed up the avenue. Papi has knitted his brows and this isn't good. He looks frustrated.

"I guess this is something we should have talked about sooner, son. I feel I owe you an apology. Ever since your mother died I've been so focused on the restaurant I figured you and Mickey would find your own paths in life without me getting in the way. I suppose that was just stupid wishful thinking."

I don't know how to respond, so, true to my wrong-thing-at-the-wrong-time nature, I go ahead and say the first thing that pops into my head. "What does it matter, anyway? I'm not going to college."

"What?" Papi says. "When did this come about? Is it the whole Isaac situation? Because I'll tell you one thing, son, I'm not letting you throw away your future like he did."

"No, it's not Isaac. It's *you*." My voice breaks. I lose my breath.

My father snaps his head back in surprise. "Me?"

We finally get to our street. My father pulls the Cadillac into the driveway and turns off the ignition. We're parked for the long haul, until we resolve this issue. I can feel it.

"I don't understand," he says. "What does this have to do with me?"

My eyes start to water. God, I can be such a girl sometimes!

"What's the matter?" Papi asks, more softly this time.

I shake my head. I can't get the words out so I start to cry instead.

"Maui, you're scaring me, son. What can be so terrible that you can't even tell your own father?" He reaches over to rub the back of my neck. "What is it?"

"I promised Mickey I'd stay behind for two years to keep you company," I say. "Just like she stuck around for two years instead of going off to college right after graduation."

Puzzled, my father raises his hand to his mouth. "But why?"

Rigoberto González

Somehow I'm able to let the answer stumble out of my mouth, my lower jaw shaking the entire time. "So you wouldn't be alone. Since Mami's not around anymore."

He shakes his head. "That's so silly," he says. "I'm grateful. And I wouldn't want to push you out if you wanted to stay. But I'm not asking you to stay. Maui, you've got a bright future ahead of you. You can make something meaningful of yourself. I'm not sure that's going to happen if you stay here. It's a hostile place for young men like you."

A tickling sensation crawls up my spine. Maybe this is it: the talk that we should have had a long time ago but were both afraid of having.

"You mean, gay." I say the word and it feels as if a heavy stone just popped out of my mouth.

"Yes," my father says. "That's what I mean."

We sit there basking in the breakthrough. It's not like he didn't know. It's not like I didn't know he knew. It's not like he didn't know that I knew he knew. But we've never talked about it openly before.

"You know I hear things all the time, even at work," my father says now that he's gotten comfortable. "Other people warn me about letting you run around with Trini. And then when Lib started showing up on television, well you can just imagine."

"Is it really that hateful out there?" I say, feeling naïve all of a sudden. My only confrontations with homophobia have been a few slurs under people's breaths at school, strange looks at the mall, and that incident with Tony Sánchez, but that wasn't really directed at me. I simply got caught in the crossfire. It's been a thousand times worse for both Trini and Lib.

"Unfortunately, yes," Papi says. "And it makes me feel terrible because I don't know how to protect you. It's one of the few times I really am sorry your mother isn't around. She would know what to do. All I can offer is to send you away, like I did at the Latino banquet."

"Is that what you're doing now by asking me to think about college?" I say, a sense of gratitude overcomes me.

"It is," Papi says. "You'll find more people like you out there, Maui. You'll fall in love and have a relationship and find happiness. Small places like this one are not going to change so quickly, even if the times are changing. Cities like these aren't ready yet for people like you and Trini and Lib."

"Then why are we still here?" I ask. "Why didn't you take me away when you knew it wasn't a safe place for me?"

"Because it's also a good place," Papi says. "There are good people in Caliente, but that doesn't mean they will be all-accepting. You were born and raised here. And this place, despite all the heartaches you've been through, made you into the good person you are. But you've outgrown us. And that's okay. Not everyone has to live where they grew up."

"You really love it here, don't you?"

"I do," Papi says. "I still have things to do here, like buy my share of the restaurant back someday. It's something I'd like to do in your mother's memory."

"I kind of love it here too," I say.

"I know that you do. But love doesn't mean you can't move away and be your own person."

I feel a renewed sense of self at that moment. My father is giving me permission to leave and find my way in the world.

"Can I ask you something?" I say.

"Sure."

"Why have you been so afraid to talk about it? You know, the whole gay thing?"

"Why have you?" my father fires back.

I smile. I'm grateful, but I also know when not to push it, so I leave it alone. At the very least we have cleared the air and now I

Rigoberto González

don't have to rethink it so often in case something else comes up, like, a boyfriend.

"We're going to have to talk about this with Mickey," I say. "I want her to know that this is a mutual agreement, not simply one of my whims."

"I'll be fine without you two," Papi says. "Besides, that's still a whole eight months from now. So much can happen in that time. So much can happen in one day."

"True that," I say. He reaches over and gives my hair a tousle.

"Are we good?" he asks.

"We're very good," I say.

As soon as I climb out of the car, a pair of headlights comes up behind us. It's Isaac's car.

"I'll be right in, Papi," I say.

Papi looks over at Isaac and waves. Isaac waves back without taking his hands off the steering wheel.

I go over to the driver's side window. "What's up?"

"Hey," Isaac says. "Care to go for a ride?"

"It's kind of late, Isaac. It's past my curfew. You remember what *that* is, right?"

"Ouch," Isaac says.

"Listen, can this wait until tomorrow? I'm having a nice moment with my father."

"Aren't you going to ask me if I remember what *that* is?"

"Ouch," I say. This whole exchange feels stupid. We used to be such good friends and never argued like this before, but now any little conflict gets in the way and becomes a battle of the put-downs.

"Just get in the car," Isaac says. "Please? We won't go anywhere, I promise. I'll even let you hold the keys."

"That won't be necessary," I say. I go around the front and take my familiar place on the front passenger's seat.

"How many conversations have we had in this car?" Isaac muses.

"Hundreds, I'm sure." Still, I look around as if it's been a while since the last time I've been inside. He's made sure not to change a thing the entire time he's been gone. The same CDs, the same copy of *Pride and Prejudice* shoved into the glove compartment without a door.

"It's what kept me going, you know," he says. "All those memories of you in here with me. It's what kept me alive."

"Don't be a drama queen," I say.

"It's true," Isaac says.

"Well you have Armando now. He'll keep you going from now on."

Isaac shakes his head. "I'm sorry about that. Armando's a good person. He has a good heart. But he's a little insecure."

"A little," I say with a laugh.

"We had a talk, though," Isaac says. "We've made some important decisions."

I look at him, hopeful that he's going to say what I want him to say: that he's coming back home, that he's coming back to school. "And...?"

"And we're going back this weekend."

"Oh." I'm unable to hide my disappointment.

"I spoke with my father about it. He's ready to get back to work on Monday. He'll have you and Jane to help out. I think he'll be fine without me. Believe me, it was more his idea than mine for him to return to work."

"I see," I say, though I'm not so keen on the idea of Mr. Dutton coming back to the store without proper rehabilitation. But I can see how it's true that not even a heart attack can keep him from his beloved Joyería.

Rigoberto González

"He promised to cut down on business hours though," Isaac adds. "And you have to make sure my father keeps that promise. For me?"

The back of my neck aches, so I reach back to give it a rub down. What I really want to say to Isaac is that his father is *his* responsibility, not mine. But my own father has just revealed to me that fathers are not the responsibilities of their sons.

"I'll keep an eye out," I say.

"Thank you, Maui," Isaac says. "You're a true friend. I love you, you know."

"I know," I say. "I love you too."

My heart begins to flutter. We've never really used those words before. And even if it's just a friend-to-friend love, there's something about saying the word out loud that forces me to take shorter breaths.

"Your neck hurt?"

"Nothing major," I manage to say. And my entire body stiffens up when Isaac reaches over to massage me.

"Geez, Maui, you've got like a third fist back here. Turn that way."

I shift my body away from him. I'm now facing the passenger side window and Isaac becomes the voice behind me and the disembodied pair of hands digging into my neck and shoulders.

"So is it true you've never slept with Armando?" I dare to say now that I'm not facing Isaac.

Isaac chuckles. "Can you keep a secret?"

I nod.

"So can I."

I laugh. "It's funny how we hardly talk about sex even though we're walking around with hard-ons instead of brains," I say.

"Well, I suppose that there are more pressing things in our world—parents, teachers, drama queens."

The Mariposa Club

As Isaac continues to massage my neck, I grow warm. We've been steering clear of any physical contact all this time that his touch suddenly feels erotic. It takes me back to that night we almost had sex. I hesitate bringing it up, but I do anyway. It's the only way I'll know his true feelings for me.

"Do you remember that time *we* came close to doing it?"

Isaac drops his hands and I turn around to look at him. The memory of it has triggered something inside him also. We're breathing heavily into each other's faces. This is it. Either I lean over and plant my lips on his. Or he leans over and plants his lips on mine. Do I stay here, waiting for one of us to make the first move? Do I cut this tender moment off at the knees? Do I stay? Do I leave? Do I decide?

"Hey," Isaac finally says. "I think I should go now."

I'm relieved that it's not me who makes the choice but I'm also disappointed that he didn't make the one I really wanted. I'm left empty-handed and flustered. "Okay," I say, awkwardly. "See you tomorrow at the store."

I open the door and shift my body toward the exit. Part of me wishes that Isaac would stop me, hold me back, bring me back down on the seat and kiss me, just kiss me. But he doesn't, and the next thing I know I'm outside the car. The car door slams shut. The ignition starts. The car drives away.

My body feels spent by the time I hit the mattress. The day has been loaded with emotion, from David, to Trini, to Armando, to Papi, to Isaac. I wish I could have recorded every exchange somehow so that I could replay each one more accurately in my head at the moment as I try to figure out what each one means, what I should have said, what I shouldn't have.

I roll over on the mattress and reach for my notebook quietly neglected in the single drawer of the lamp table. This had been the school psychologist's gift to me soon after my mother died. I was supposed to express in written words what I could not express in spoken ones. Every page remains blank, but not for lack of inspiration. I simply froze at the thought of someone opening it up and discovering what was really going through my head. I suppose holding things in, like remaining closeted, is one form of survival, though not the best way in the long run. Instead of revealing anything, I simply kept a photograph hidden at the center of the journal like a bookmark.

The picture shows my mother at the age of eighteen. I took it out of the family album soon after she died and though its absence is noticeable my father has never asked for it back. She looks so wise beyond her years, as if she has been through so much already, that nothing that crosses her path after this photograph will surprise her. But that wasn't true. Many more surprises awaited her.

Each time I look at it I see myself growing more and more into this image of my mother. And I'm reminded that I have survived every day I have already lived, and that there are many more days, both welcomed and unwelcomed, yet to come.

Bullet

Saturday. The week before Christmas. Winter recess is only a few days away but the flurry of youth—loud and careless in the mall—suggests that vacation mode has already begun. Even I'm feeling a little detached from all things academic. Math? Science? None of that seems to fit with the contagious festive spirit around me. The Holiday Village Arts & Crafts Fair gives the already crowded wings another layer of activity to be reckoned with: small booths and tables peddle everything from tamales to artsy stockings, from wall clocks to Mexican blouses embroidered with Christmas colors. The loudspeakers play the conventional holiday tunes and every once in a while one of the customers at Joyería Dutton hums or sings along. Celie walks around with a red Santa cap, but doesn't bother to tone down the Goth makeup, so she's looking like something out of a Christmas horror flick. But on her it's the hat that looks out of place.

Jane blurts out, "During my break, I'm buying one of those purses decorated with mistletoe." She too has been seized by the spending spirit. "Maybe I'll get holiday socks to match. Maybe I'll get a little jewelry box from Mexico—they're so pretty. I won't ruin it by putting in jewelry though—not from *our* store. What can I put in it?" she ponders. "I know, maybe I can buy a holiday—"

"Hey, Christmas Jane," Isaac says. "Do you mind getting Mr. Dutton a bottle of water or something? It's getting warm here fast."

Jane replies, indignant, "Why don't you send Maui?"

"Because I asked *you*. Move!"

"Yes, master," Jane says. She rolls her eyes and then holds out her hand. "Money?"

Isaac digs into his pocket and hands Jane a five dollar bill. "And bring back the change," he says as she walks away.

Since the morning, Mr. Dutton has been in the back room going over the paperwork that's been sitting neglected on his desk the entire week. He hasn't said anything about Isaac's leaving again, but then again, I suspect Mr. D's too preoccupied with his store to worry about his errant gay son.

Isaac and I have not had time to revisit the moment we had the night before, but we've also been avoiding direct eye contact. When he needs to tell me something he simply says it, but nothing further. With all the coming and going of clientele, it's more likely that the conversation—if there needs to be a conversation—will happen after closing time. The only thing I know for sure is that Armando has returned to LA to tend to his own business and that he's expecting Isaac to return to him tomorrow.

That means that today is my last day with Isaac, and that we will spend the whole day together but not communicating with each other. In a way I'm grateful. It'll give me a chance to formulate how I want to express that I'm still afraid for him, that I think it's a mistake to go back out there with this Armando guy who

Rigoberto González

can be a real asshole, that I want him to stay here with me, and that maybe, perhaps, we can be more than friends.

Yet I suspect that no amount of pleading is going to change his mind. I have to get used to my days without Isaac again. But at least now I know what it's like—I have lived them before. And though he entrusts me with his new cell phone number I can't imagine that I will call that often. For what? To bore him with my uninteresting high school dramas? *Hey, Isaac, guess what happened in third period today?* Wrong. But then again, I can't imagine that he'll be calling me much either to tell me about those things that are only interesting to grown-ups like dinner parties and home repairs. Not that that's what Armando's all about, but I can only speculate. I mean, well, I just know that it's not my life. And deep down inside I also know that Isaac's got a lot of issues to work out before he'd be willing to try out a relationship with someone like me. Armando's easier: He's already an adult. Me, I'm barely fumbling forward into adulthood, just like Isaac.

As a respite to all the things swirling in my head, Maddy and Snake walk hand in hand into the jewelry store, both of them looking cheery.

"Hello, there," I say. By now I don't think they make such an odd couple. With matching glows on their faces, their shoulders back and heads held up high for a change, they look like they were made for each other. It's sweet, actually.

"Hello, Maui," Snake says. "Madeleine and I have come to check out the engagement rings?"

Maddy lets out a giggle and presses her open palm on Snake's chest. "Oh, Walter," she says.

It's going to take more time than I thought to get used the new Maddy and Snake. Madeleine and Walter, that is. Still, customers are customers and I give them the spiel on Mr. Dutton's layaway and credit plans, plus the "no down payment" special and the Christmas season discount. And then I reel them in by pointing out the range of designs, from the simple and understated to the loud and clear.

"Let your finger itch for one of these," I say.

When I pull out a showcase Maddy beams. She's looking more feminine than I've ever seen her as she sports a new manicure and hairdo. Her pink nails tap on the glass with anticipation as Snake takes the first ring and slides it onto her finger.

It's an emotional moment for Maddy, so I discreetly step away and let the couple have their fun with the rings.

"Wow," Isaac says. "I look away for one minute and Maddy blossoms into a girl and Snake blossoms into a...human."

"You don't know the half of it," I say. "But I'm very happy for them. Since Snake's still alive I venture to guess that Sheriff Johnson took the news well."

"About their engagement?"

It dawns on me that Isaac doesn't know about Maddy's pregnancy. In the old days I would've just dished right then and there. But Isaac's no longer part of the circle, so this is news not worth whispering into his ears. So I keep it to myself.

"Yes," I lie. "About their engagement."

While Maddy and Snake get swallowed up in their private two-person moment, I'm hailed to help a lady match a filigree pendant with the filigree earrings she's already wearing.

"How does this look?" she asks, holding the necklace against her chest.

"Maybe," I say. I reach down and offer her another possibility. "Try this one."

She poses with the second necklace. And as I'm trying to coordinate her jewelry, I catch sight of Lib in the background, hauling a folding table and a tote bag. For the next few minutes, I shift my eyes from the customer to Lib, positioning his renegade table and *The Mariposa Club: A Gay/Straight Alliance* sign. That little lawbreaker: he goes ahead with his kamikaze activism, setting up

Rigoberto González

without official permission. And as soon as he's finished arranging pamphlets on the table, he starts to shout through the verses of "Rudolph the Red-Nosed Reindeer."

"Get your information here, people!" he says. "The Mariposa Club: A Gay/Straight Alliance!"

"Excuse me," I tell the filigree lady. I motion to Jane with my finger.

"Yes, master?" Jane says.

"I don't have time for this, Jane," I say. "Can you take over for me here? I need to step away for a minute."

"Go ahead. I've got nothing better to do."

I ignore other pleas for assistance and make my way through the crowd to get to Lib.

"Pamphlet, sir?" Lib says, holding one out to me in his hand.

"Lib," I say. "You're going to get kicked out. By your own sister."

"I'm fine with that," he says. "As long as I make my presence known, I'll have done my job."

People walk by looking askance and confused at the large sign with the telltale pink triangles. Lib holds out his pamphlets but he gets no more attention here than he did when we sat at the high school club fair. One passerby slaps the pamphlet out of Lib's hand.

"Hey!" I say. But that's all I can say. This isn't the high school. We can't depend on the threat of suspension to keep hostility at bay. I catch sight of Celie in the distance as she helps organize the Santa Claus line full of hyperactive children. I want to run over there and tell her, but that would be betraying Lib since Celie will be forced to close down his squatter's booth.

"Gay/Straight Alliance!" Lib shouts.

"Lib, this is crazy," I say.

"Maui, if you're not going to be part of this movement then get out of my way. You're blocking my sign."

The Mariposa Club

As more people pass by, the looks on their faces range from puzzled to outraged. Or at least that's how I see it. I'm aware that my own state of distress is skewing my perception. All I can think about is the conversation I had last night with my father.

"Be careful, Lib," I continue.

"Relax, Maui. What are you so afraid of? I'm in a public space. What's the worse that can happen?" I drop my head and give him the "you're joking, right?" look.

"Well, if you get into trouble, I'm just over there," I say. With that weak assurance I make my way back to the jewelry store.

Maddy calls to me. "We're ready, Maui." Snake leans in to give her a hug.

"Did you find something you both liked?" I ask.

"We sure did," Maddy says. She holds up a ring with a pink diamond.

"I'll have Mr. Dutton draw up the financial paperwork and I'll be right with you," I say.

I go into the back room. Mr. Dutton sits at his desk, tallying up figures on an adding machine. He's so old fashioned he resists using the computer as much as he can.

"I've got a nice sale for you," I tell him.

"Excellent, excellent," Mr. Dutton says. "How's Jane doing?"

"Oh, she's a pistol," I say.

I drop the paperwork and let him input the merchandise information on the computer in the back while I take Snake's data at the front. *Walter Eugene Simmons*, I write.

Isaac comes up to me. "Trini wants you."

I'm so focused on my task that I don't take my eyes off the forms. "Is she on the phone? Tell her I'll call her back later."

"Nope," Isaac says. "She's over there with her boyfriend."

I look up, look around. "Boyfriend?"

"Yoo-hoo, Maui," Trini calls out to me. She stands very close to Davy Wavy.

Rigoberto González

"Good grief," I say. "Excuse me a minute, guys. In the meantime, fill this out here, here, here and sign here."

I hand Snake a pen and then walk toward Trini. In the background I can hear someone complaining, "Take this sick shit out of the mall, there are children here!"

"Hello, Maui," Trini says, turning her face away. "We came to clear things up."

"Trini," I say. "Forget about all that, Lib's going to get his ass kicked."

"Oh, him?" Trini says. "He'll be fine. We're at the mall."

An angry parent ushers his two children away from Lib. Crisis averted.

"Trini," I say. "I don't have time for this, I'm working!"

"It won't take long," she says. "David wants to tell you something. Tell him, David."

David looks at me with a hint of malice on his face. This is all a game to him. Suddenly I have the urge to slap him.

"Maui, it's no good between us. Trini is the one I want to be with." David delivers the line so deadpan it's as if this fantasy they're both fabricating is real.

"What? What are you talking about?" I say.

"He's dumping your ass, you trinket store hussy!" Trini says. "From now on, talk to the hand because I've *got* a man!"

The jewelry store suddenly goes quiet and all heads turn toward us. In that silence we can all hear Lib loud and clear: "Join the Mariposa Club: A Gay/Straight Alliance!" And then suddenly all heads turns toward Lib.

"A gay/straight alliance?" someone says. "What's that? A sex club?"

Isaac walks toward us. "What the hell is going on here? Do you mind taking your lovers' quarrel somewhere else, Trini?"

"Don't worry," she says, linking her arm to David's. "We're through here."

The Mariposa Club

"Are they a couple?" someone in the store says. "Wow."

"This is disgusting!" a man in front of Lib's table yells out.

"Lib!" Celie calls out as she rushes over. "Are you trying to get me fired? What do you think you're doing?"

Mr. Dutton pops his head out from behind the back room door. "The Simmons paperwork is done!" he announces.

"This place is full of fags!" someone else yells out. This from one of Los Calis. Tony Sánchez stands tall among his dope-dealing cohorts.

"Watch your language," Celie warns. "This is a family space."

"Yeah," the man in front of Lib's table scoffs. "That why's this freak is shoving his homosexual propaganda in our kids' faces?"

"This is educational material, sir," Lib insists, self-assured. "Your children could certainly use it."

"You shut up, freak!" the man says, raising his arm at Lib.

"You need to calm down, sir," Calie says. In the meantime, the curious crowd gathered around the scene of the conflict has grown, everyone watching intently.

"That's the faggot that got you expelled," one of Tony's buddies says to Tony.

"Faggot," the other one says. "Well, kick his ass, Tony."

"All right, guys," Celie says. "You know the drill. You're being too disruptive so you need to vacate the premises."

"And take this one out, too," the angry man says, pointing at Lib.

"I'm taking care of this, sir, not you," Celie says. She then turns to Lib. "Bring this table down, Lib."

"Figures she knows his name. They look alike," the angry man says, looking around for approval. Los Calis burst into exaggerated laughter.

"Take him out, dude," one of Los Calis says to Tony. "This is your chance."

"I'm taking *you* guys out," Celie says to Los Calis.

Rigoberto González

"*This* is the one you should be removing," the angry man says, pointing at Lib, though he takes a step closer to Celie.

Celie holds out her hand. "Let me do my job, sir. Please keep your distance." She begins to speak into her walkie-talkie, but she's not even half-way through a sentence when the man knocks the walkie-talkie out of her hand. It falls to the ground and shatters.

"Oops!" the angry man says, though his intent was clear.

"Oh, shit," I hear Isaac say. "Dad, call the police." Mr. Dutton scurries to the back room.

"Take *her* out, dude," one of Los Calis says to the angry man.

"You all need to back the hell up!" It's Maddy. She cuts through the crowd and confronts the angry man and Los Calis with her hands on her hips.

"Madeleine," Snake says, but his plea collapses against the adrenaline rush that's sweeping through the air.

"Maddy, stay back please," Celie says. Even through her make-up it's obvious how nervous she is. She's lost control of the situation.

"I'm leaving now, okay, look," Lib says as he begins to shove pamphlets back into the tote bag. "I'm picking up my things and leaving. Everything's okay."

"Don't let him get away," one of Los Calis says, egging Tony on.

"David," Trini says. "Do something."

"*Me*?" David says with a nervous laugh. "I don't want to get involved. I don't know these people."

"They're my friends," Trini says, trying to push David forward, but David resists.

"I'm out of here," David says, shaking Trini's hand off. "I'm not getting killed because of a bunch of freaks."

"David!" Trini yells out, going after him. "David, come back here!"

The Mariposa Club

Spotting Trini, one of Los Calis says, "Oh, look, there's the biggest fag of all."

All this time Tony says nothing, but keeps turning his head to wherever his attention gets directed. Other people keep looking around also, at Lib, then at Celie, then at Trini, as if for the first time, as if they've suddenly realized that the weirdos are walking among them.

"That's that kid from the TV," someone says, finally recognizing Lib.

"Sick piece of shit," someone mutters.

"Sick shit," Tony echoes. And that's when the mood turns another shade darker. Los Calis have finally gotten to Tony.

"Tony," I call out, but he doesn't hear me. I'm trapped behind a wall of bodies, though I don't feel particularly inspired to move in closer.

"You're disgusting," Tony says to Lib. Even from a distance I can see the madness in his eyes.

"Hey, back off!" Celie says, standing in front of Lib.

"Sick! Disgusting!" Tony yells.

"But you're one of us," Lib says to Tony. The statement comes out so softly, but everyone hears it.

"What's he saying?" Los Calis chime in. "Is he calling you a faggot, Tony?"

"I'll take them all out," Tony says, sticking his hand inside his jacket.

"Yeah! Yeah!" Los Calis cry out. "Take all the freaks out!"

"Yes!" the angry man says. "Yes!"

"Tony!" I scream out and for a brief moment Tony turns his head to look for me. He's looking in my direction but he can't see me.

"Do it! Do it!" Los Calis chant.

The entire scene seems unreal for the next few seconds as everyone stands still, the suspense all consuming, as if somebody

Rigoberto González

has forgotten their next line, as if somebody has missed their cue. We all stand frozen—confused, shocked, numb—waiting, waiting, waiting for the next move. Even the holiday music seems to have gone mute.

And then, all at once we know what to do when Tony Sánchez pulls out a gun. When he flashes the shiny metal it's as if he has detonated dynamite because bodies all around react, collapsing and jumping at the unmistakable obscenity of the object. The panic pushes the crowd like a tsunami and I find myself thrown back by a pair of bodies trying to pass right through me. The screams and shrieks ricochet inside the unfortunate acoustics of the mall and the anxiety doubles.

When my head hits the floor, at first I think that *that's* what caused the bang. And for a split second I'm distracted by the strange sound of it. It's funny almost. *Bang!* as my skull strikes the carpet. *Bang!* the echo, and then the sensation of something oozing out of my nose. I reach up to touch it. I bring my bloodied fingers close to my eyes. And when I hear someone shout, "Someone got shot! Someone got shot!" I'm convinced that that "someone" is me.

My body grows cold and limp. My head spins, my sight becomes blurry. I've been shot. Well, this is an unexpected turn of events. I won't be able to graduate from high school or go to college or lose my virginity because I've been shot. I won't be able to say goodbye to Mickey, or Papi, or Trini, or Lib, or Isaac because I've been shot. I'm hoping Isaac or Lib will clean out all of my pornographic downloads on the computer before my father gets to them. Maybe Boozely will allow a plaque to be drilled into the Queer Planter in my name. *In Loving Memory of Mauricio "Passion Flower" Gutiérrez. He got shot.*

I always imagined death to be more sudden, more symbolic even—the light at the end of the tunnel, the spirits of those who departed before me welcoming me to the afterlife. I can hear bells, but it's only the jingling of the Christmas song in the loud-speakers. Even in transition I can't shake the mall music.

I shift my eyes a little, attempting to find Mami with her angel wings and halo. As the mist clears, I think I see her. She hovers right above me.

"Maui," her voice says.

"Mami?" I say. And then everything goes dark and quiet. Just like that. The silence isn't frightening or cold or unsettling. It's just empty. I'm a blank now, surrendered to the calm and sooth-ing bodiless afterlife.

"Maui," another voice says. I feel a slight slap against my cheek and I'm stunned back to consciousness by the sight of Isaac look-ing down at me. "Maui, are you okay? You blacked out for a min-ute there."

"I didn't get shot?" I ask in disbelief.

"No, Maui, you didn't get shot," Isaac says, but his face looks pale with distress.

"What happened then?" I ask.

Isaac only shakes his head. Now uglier things are running through my mind: Maddy? Celie? Trini? Lib? I look around but people are standing all around me blocking my view. Snake? Mr. Dutton? Jane? The mystery pumps some strength in me and with some help from Isaac I'm able to get up.

Sheriff Johnson is at the scene and is comforting Maddy. Snake holds on to her tightly. The sheriff places his hand over Snake's shoulder and then walks over to Celie, who's lost her Santa Claus hat in the scuffle. Los Calis stand handcuffed and closely guard-ed by the assisting police officers. Mr. Dutton wraps both arms around Jane, who cries with her face against his chest.

"Where's Trini?" I say. "Where's Lib?"

The paramedics are also on the scene. One stands over Lib, ad-ministering oxygen. A few feet away from Lib lies a body covered completely by a white blanket soaking up blood.

Rigoberto González

"Oh, my God!" I scream out and rush toward the body.

"Maui!" Isaac calls out, but I won't stop. I'm devastated that the last time I spoke to Trini I was such an asshole. Why couldn't I have been a better friend? Why couldn't I have given her my undivided, uncompromised attention?

"Trini! Trini!" I call out. One of the police officers tries to stop me but I wrestle my body out of his grip.

Lib removes the mask from his face and he says something but I can't hear it. My mind is seized with anger and grief and regret. I dive down to the floor and land next to the body. Before anyone can stop me, I lift the sheet to uncover the face.

"Maui, step back, please!" Celie orders. She puts her hand under my arm and I let her lift me off the ground.

"I don't understand," I say, my voice cracking. "How?"

"Come on," Celie says. "Keep my little brother company while we take care of business here."

The paramedics wrap the body in a body bag, load it on a gurney and remove it from the mall. One of them comes up to Lib.

"You okay now, buddy?" he asks. "Or do you need to come with us?"

"No, thank you," Lib says. "I think I can breathe on my own now."

"How about you, son?" the paramedic asks me.

I rub my bloody nostril. "I'm good," I say.

The paramedic takes the oxygen tank away. Soon after, the crowds begin to disperse, except for a few curious onlookers who can't get enough of the tragedy.

"How did it happen?" I ask Lib.

Lib shakes his head. "It all happened so quickly. Sheriff Johnson tackled him down and the gun went off. But Tony wasn't pointing it at me. He was pointing it toward himself."

"Poor Tony," I say. My heart feels the pang of sadness for the boy who kissed me in elementary school, and who probably would've kissed me again if he hadn't lost his way. It makes me want to leave this place that much sooner. "And what about Trini?"

Lib shrugs his shoulders. I'm about to check around for Trini, when I catch sight of her, walking down the wing with all her attitude intact.

I jump up and hug her as soon as she's within reach. "You bitch, you gave me a scare!"

"Take note, girls," Trini says. "We will no longer be patronizing this crime-infested establishment. Gun fights inside, tire slashing outside."

"Tire slashing?" I ask.

Trini nods. "Davy Wavy's ride just got triple crippled," she says. "I wonder who he could've pissed off *that* much."

"Geez, Trini," Lib said. "You mean you were out there avenging your honor while we're in here dodging bullets?"

"Hey," Isaac says. "We're closing the store down for the rest of the afternoon and I'm taking Jane home."

"How is she?" I ask.

"Still upset," Isaac says. "She's not supposed to be seeing things like this."

"None of us are," Lib says.

"Go on ahead," Trini says. "Paulina Rubio and I can give these girls a ride home."

"Hey, so is this goodbye?" I say, slightly taken aback by the abrupt conclusion to the reunion. "You leave tomorrow."

Isaac nods. "I do. Some goodbye, huh?"

"Well, I'm not in any kind of party mood," I say, "But maybe we can all see you off tomorrow morning."

"You don't have to do that," Isaac says. My chest deflates. "It's not like I'm leaving forever."

Forever. The word plops in the center of our circle, shattering to pieces. It just might be that, though—forever. And Isaac doesn't

Rigoberto González

seem to be affected by it as much as the rest of us. He realizes this and tries to make amends.

"Well, how about a group hug before I leave, just to be grateful that none of us got hurt," Isaac says.

We gather around. When we tighten the circle with an embrace I can't help but tear up. The gesture feels empty. This *is* goodbye. Maybe forever. Maybe not. The uncertainty of the future is what allows us to look forward to the next week, to the next month, to the next year. But I do know—the coolness of the group hug tells me so—that tomorrow there will no getting together to say goodbye to Isaac.

Exhausted, we will all sleep in the next day, and then we'll call each other later, disappointed but not all that surprised that Isaac drove off to LA without ceremony or fanfare. But we also know that deep down Isaac prefers it this way as well—to ride away quietly, leaving behind Caliente and all its citizens in that old bookshelf he will call his past.

"I'll see you girls around," Isaac says, and then walks away.

Lib sighs and says, "Well, at least winter break is almost here. All I want to do is hibernate."

"Hey, so, we can't just leave it like this, you know," I say.

Trini raises her brow. "Like what?"

"You know, with Tony's death," I say. "He was one of us, in more ways than one. You know that."

"What are you suggesting? That we show up at his funeral to drape his coffin with a rainbow flag?" Trini says. "I'm sure Los Calis wouldn't appreciate that."

"I don't know, something," I say. "It just feels so disrespectful letting go of his death like this."

"I think Maui's right," Lib says. "We can do something for ourselves in his memory. He's the one who didn't make it out of closet or out of Caliente."

"I suppose," Trini says, not completely convinced. "Well, how about tomorrow night at my house, since I can't leave Aunt Carmen alone for long. You two think you can make it to my house all right?"

"I can get Celie to drop me off," Lib says.

"I can walk over after the store closes," I say.

"Then it's settled," Trini says. "All right girls, let's get out of this hell hole. We don't call it the Lame View Mall for nothing."

We head toward the exit and push open the door.

Rigoberto González

Mr. Dutton decides not to open the jewelry store the next day so I spend the entire Sunday morning watching music videos. I avoid the news since the television continues to reel with excitement about the shooting at the mall. Only once do I stumble across the news, and it holds my attention because the camera decides to show a photograph of "seventeen-year-old Antonio Sánchez, Caliente Valley High School senior," looking cheerful and innocent. He was a cute boy, and in another context, perhaps he could've been part of our Mariposa Club. In another reality maybe he could've sat with us at the Queer Planter and elbowed us whenever there was a sighting of Mr. Trotter. Instead, he's reduced to a headline, another cautionary tale of youth gone astray. The memory of his body lying on the bloodied floor at the mall moves me. I shed a heavy tear and wipe it slowly off my cheek with an open hand.

"Maui, are you okay?" Mickey asks.

I rub my eyes. "Sorry. I didn't know you were here."

She sits down next to me. "Hey. It's all right. Tears are fine. Even from boys."

"Please," I say. She hugs me anyway and kisses my forehead.

"I'm so glad nothing terrible happened," she says.

I correct her. "But something terrible *did* happen. To Tony."

"But he was some punk," Mickey says. "He was a gang member and a dope-dealer. Of course it wasn't going to end well for him."

I can't let it go that easily. "He was my age. He attended my school."

"But he wasn't like you, Maui," Mickey says. "You're here to do *good* things. Not bad ones."

I don't want to argue with my sister. But I also want her to leave me alone. I spent all last night getting smothered with sympathy by my father, who came home horrified after news about the shooting at the mall reached Las Cazuelas.

"Hey, I need my space," I say, softly. "Do you mind?"

"No, not at all," Mickey says. "I'll be in my room straightening my hair. Just knock if you need anything." She kisses me on the forehead again and then leaves the living room.

I sink down on the couch and close my eyes. Tony Sánchez will live in my memory having three faces: the hateful one he wore to survive among Los Calis, the sad one looking at me from the corner of the library, and the defeated one I saw when I lifted the white sheet at the mall.

The only other dead body I've ever seen is my own mother's. And yesterday I confirmed something: It's not true that a lifeless body looks at peace. A lifeless body looks vacant. It's as if its personality has been erased, and the face, disconnected entirely from the living, goes empty. That's why it becomes so important to be remembered, and to leave something behind so that the living will be able to say that it mattered that you were once here.

Rigoberto González

That's why the living have to remember and keep the memory of what is lost sacred.

So this is where it stands so far: I worry for Isaac Dutton, dropping out of high school and driving off to the big city with an older man. I worry for Trinidad Ramos, our resident gender-bender who can never step into a room without immediate notice. I worry for Liberace García, Goth activist. And then there's me, Mauricio Gutiérrez, still uncertain about how I'm going to make a difference while I'm still breathing. Maybe there's something to be said about Lib's mission after all. Or maybe my destiny—my life, my boyfriend—awaits me beyond the Caliente Valley border, in some distant city I have yet to imagine. Poor Tony didn't get that chance. And even though I'm still seventeen, I know now that I can't say I've got all the time in the world.

I curl up on the couch and turn the television off. It's almost noon. Another Sunday of my life is passing me by. So I better make it count.

Feeling generous today, Mickey drops me off at Trini's. I step inside the house without knocking and walk in on Lib and Aunt Carmen having tea in the living room. One of her old Diva records plays on the record player. I recognize the unmistakable voice of Lola Beltrán.

"Welcome," Lib says. He leans toward Aunt Carmen and yells: "It's Maui!"

Aunt Carmen nods her head. "So nice of you to visit," she says, barely audible.

I bend down to kiss Aunt Carmen on the cheek. She smells like a fresh bouquet. I'm pleased to see she looks so much better than she did a few months ago. Trini has been caring for her nicely, making sure she's always made-up and well-dressed.

"Where's Trini?" I ask Lib.

"You rang?" Trini says. She walks in wearing a black blouse and a red skirt. "You like?" she says, twirling around. "It's my Sunday-go-to-church attire with a little cocktail dress thrown in."

"Sure," I say, smiling. "Me, I'll always be a jeans and t-shirt kind of guy."

"And that's how I like you, Passion Flower," Trini says. "Simple, but not plain."

"Well," Lib says as soon as we're all seated around the coffee table. "This was probably the most eventful semester of our high school years."

"You're telling me," I say. "And we've still got one more to go before graduation."

Trini scoffs. "Graduation into what? Into the streets of this horrible society?"

"Graduation into the unpredictable life," Lib says.

Unsettled by the silence that follows, Trini steps in: "Oh, come on! Let's not get too reflective. We're seventeen"—she then turns and nods at Lib—"and younger. We've got our whole lives ahead of us."

The pit of my stomach grows uneasy. No more taking life for granted, I want to tell them, but I don't want put a damper on Trini's sudden spurt of positive thinking.

"You're right," Lib says. "And something inside me tells me that the best is yet to come."

"I like the sound of that," Trini says with a suggestive wink.

"Well, before it gets any more raunchy," I say. "Let's do our ceremony."

There's nothing planned, exactly. We just kind of make it up as we go along. First, we help Trini take Aunt Carmen to bed because she's falling asleep. Then we light a few candles, dim the lights, put on some soft music, and bust out with Aunt Carmen's fancy flutes. We fill them up with ginger ale that we pretend is champagne.

Rigoberto González

"Go ahead, Maui," Trini says as soon as we're sitting down again.

"Me? You're the one that always has something to say."

"True," Trini says. "But this is your idea. Besides, if it isn't sass it's not going to come out of my mouth."

I take a deep breath and begin: "All right. This toast, the first official function of the Mariposa Club, is in memory of Tony Sánchez, honorary member, post-mortem. May he be remembered by those who loved him, may he not be forgotten by those who knew him, may his death be a reminder to us all that we should be who we want to be, because life is short."

We raise our flutes, clink, and then take a sip.

"I'd like to make another toast," Lib says.

"Sure," I say.

"Let's also put our glasses together in honor of the absent member of the Fierce Foursome," Lib says. "To Isaac, our queer sister, we wish her luck on her early journey into adulthood. May she send plenty of postcards so that it won't be a complete shock to us when we finally get there. May she be happier and practice safe sex."

"Okay..." I say. We raise our flutes, clink, and then take a sip.

"And let's not neglect ourselves," Trini says. She raises her glass. "Let us toast each other. May the fairy dust always rain over our heads. May our claws always be flawlessly manicured. May we always shine on the runway. And may we never let a man come between us again."

Lib narrows his eyes as he looks at Trini askance and then smiles.

"I'll toast to that," I say. And we do.

"Now let us put our glasses down, girls," Trini says. "And close the ceremony with our sign."

"Sign?" Lib says.

The Mariposa Club

"Cross your hands over your tits," Trini says, and we follow her directions. "Lock your thumbs. Now flutter your fingers. We are the Mariposa Club!"

We unleash our laughter, though inside I feel another knot. I got the first one when my mother died, the second after Isaac left. They never go away. So I don't let them get me down because I have a feeling I will be collecting many more in my future.

We're butterflies all right, except we're still strengthening our wings inside the cocoon we call Caliente, the small mostly-Mexican town that still needs to grow up as well. But, like Papi says, it's *our* town. And after all that's happened, I'm more determined than ever to do some good here before I fly away.

Rigoberto González

Acknowledgments

With deep gratitude to Lethe Press and Steve Berman for giving *The Mariposa Club* a second chance.

Rigoberto González is the author of eight books of poetry and prose, and the editor of *Camino del Sol: Fifteen Years of Latina and Latino Writing*. The recipient of Guggenheim and NEA fellowships, winner of the American Book Award, and The Poetry Center Book Award, he writes a Latino book column for the *El Paso Times* of Texas. He is contributing editor for *Poets and Writers* magazine, on the Board of Directors of the National Book Critics Circle, and is Associate Professor of English at Rutgers—Newark, State University of New Jersey.

LaVergne, TN USA
04 December 2010
207252LV00006B/46/P